Penguin Books
The Open House

Michael Innes is the pseudonym of
J. I. M. Stewart, who has been Student of Christ
Church, Oxford, since 1949. He was born in
1906 and was educated at Edinburgh Academy
and Oriel College, Oxford. He was lecturer in
English at the University of Leeds from 1930
to 1935, when he became Jury Professor of
English in the University of Adelaide, South
Australia. From 1946 to 1948 he was Lecturer
in English at Queen's University, Belfast. He
has published books on English literature and
novels under his own name, as well as detective
novels and broadcast scripts as Michael Innes.
He is married and has five children.

Michael Innes

The Open House

Penguin Books

Penguin Books Ltd, Harmondsworth,
Middlesex, England
Penguin Books Australia Ltd, Ringwood,
Victoria, Australia

First published by Victor Gollancz 1972
Published in Penguin Books 1973

Made and printed in Great Britain by
C. Nicholls & Company Ltd
Set in Intertype Times

Part One Around Midnight

Chapter One

The sudden immobilizing of his car hadn't much discomposed John Appleby, but the subsequent failure of his electric torch was another matter.

Not that what had happened to the car wasn't absurd enough to make anybody cross. The night was uncommonly dark and the road unfrequented; he had neither overtaken nor met any other vehicle for miles; there seemed to be no nocturnal pedestrianism or bicycling in this part of the countryside, so that his powerful headlights had the verges comfortably to themselves. Then suddenly there had been the tail-lights of a slow-moving van ahead of him and the brow of a hill beyond. So he had slowed, and changed down to third. Only the gears somehow hadn't engaged, and in a moment he knew why. He was waving the gear-lever in air.

It hadn't been difficult to steer on to a reliable-looking grass verge, and there he had come to a halt and investigated. He was in neutral, he found, and in neutral he was going to remain. The confounded lever had broken off close to the gearbox. There was nothing whatever to be done.

Appleby switched on the light above his head, and regarded the useless object he was left with. Grasped in reverse, it could be employed to crack a dangerously violent criminal on the head. With its knob suitably padded, it might serve a painter as a maulstick. But these were idle speculations. Appleby chucked the thing behind him, and got out a map. What he had to find was a tolerable pub. The car wasn't of a make that was exactly thick on the ground; in fact it was a recent acquisition of Lady Appleby's, and rather exotic. A new gear-lever would have to come from goodness knew where. Since the hour was not far short of midnight, Appleby was booked for a strange bed. He located his approximate position, which certainly seemed to be in notably uninhabited terrain. But not much more than a mile ahead, a little way down a side-road of a minor sort to the right, was inscribed the word *Inn*. It seemed in an isolated situation for an hostelry; there didn't appear to be so much as a hamlet nearby. But he could either get a room there, or make a nuisance of himself until they found him a hired car. Appleby rummaged in his suitcase, shoved a few necessary articles into a small bag, locked up the disgraced vehicle, and took to the road.

There was no moon, but the heavens did show a faint powdering of stars. Although he had a torch in his pocket – a small but powerful torch – it didn't at first occur to him that he would need it except to consult his map or read a signpost. English darkness is seldom so entire as to render an alert walker hopelessly blundering on an unimpeded road. And to walk with confidence under such conditions can be rather fun.

But in fact it *was* very dark. *The blanket of the dark,* Appleby said to himself as he moved cautiously forward. *Nor heaven peep through the blanket of the dark to cry 'Hold, hold!'* One of Appleby's academically inclined children had once solemnly assured his father that here was a textual corruption, and that Shakespeare had really written *blank height of the dark*. But that was nonsense, Appleby told himself now. The tactile quality of a blanket was just what, in this Tartarean blackness, his own nose felt uncomfortably up against. So he switched on his torch after all, and moved more rapidly forward. He would need it, in any case, if he was not to miss that unnoticeable side-road on his right. And if a car came along behind him it might help him to get a lift.

It was some ten minutes later that the torch failed. He fiddled with it, but to no effect. The battery couldn't thus abruptly have exhausted itself. The trouble was probably in the little bulb. One ought always to carry a spare bulb. This time, and at a halt in the darkness, Sir John Appleby actually was upset. Long ago – long before he had become Sir John – he had let his life depend on an electric torch more than once. He had also let it depend on toy pistols, knotted sheets, implausible disguises, ridiculous bluffs. But at the moment, somehow, torches seemed almost symbolically important. A policeman, however retired, who permitted a torch to let him down like this was slipping up badly on the elements of his craft.

Dismissing this nonsense from his head, Appleby got under way again. But now he was going to be in real difficulty. It was his guess that, in a middle-of-the-road way, he could forge ahead indefinitely without coming a cropper; something that appeared mere instinct, but that in fact must be the ghost of sight, was going to guide his steps. But sensing that side-road was another matter. To manage that he must keep very close to the right-hand verge. It wasn't clear to him that this mightn't at any moment tumble him into a ditch. So perhaps his best plan was to abandon the idea of making that inn, and keep straight on until he came on some other inhabited place. He'd better take a look at his map by matchlight. It seemed inconceivable that the road should be totally devoid of human dwellings for more than three or four miles at the most. But he'd have a look. He ought to have checked on the point at the start. He took the map from his pocket, and felt for his matches. He hadn't any. And instantly he could see, almost like a hallucination, the dashboard of his car, with his pipe, tobacco-pouch and matchbox conveniently ranged on the little shelf above it. Appleby's displeasure with himself grew. He meditated briefly a return to the car, and waiting in it until something came along – which might conceivably not be till daylight. But this seemed defeatism. He moved slowly forward.

He found the side-road – or thought he did – after all. The illuminated dial of his wrist-watch told him it was still twenty minutes short of midnight, and the inn couldn't now be more than two or three hundred yards away. Appleby was not at all tired, but he did suddenly feel uncommonly hungry. He had been driving most of the day, and his last wayside meal had been a light one early in the evening. He supposed that even at this hour a pub would find him bread and cheese. If he spent the night there he would count as a resident and even be allowed a drink. He found himself moving forward at what was almost a reckless pace.

It was now darker still, and this seemed to be because even the ineffective stars had vanished. Or they had vanished except for a few straight overhead. Appleby realized that this humble little road – or lane – to nowhere in particular was either passing through woodland (of which he could recall no indication on the map) or lined on either side with trees of a considerable height. This was the only explanation of what had happened in the heavens.

Closing-time having arrived more than an hour ago, it was likely enough that the people at the pub would have gone to bed. Certainly there was no glimmer of light ahead – any more than behind or to either side of him. He hadn't seen any such glimmer, indeed, since leaving his car. If the pub proved to be untenanted – long since closed down through lack of custom in this seemingly unpopulated region – he would be reduced to breaking into an outbuilding and burrowing into straw, if there *was* any straw. But if it had tenants he certainly wouldn't make any bones about rousing them up.

The night was very still. His ear, it occurred to him, was having to get along on as short commons as his eye. Rural writers are fond of enumerating the multitudinous sounds which even the most silent-seeming night will offer to the instructed listener: hedgehogs puffing across the path, Appleby thought, and worms wriggling beneath the sod. But he had himself distinguished nothing except a train in the distance and the hoot of a single discontented owl. That, and his own footfalls. His own footfalls . . . Appleby listened to them again now. He halted, and stirred at the surface beneath his tread with an exploring toe. He stooped, and let his fingers confirm the message. This was no sort of by-road or country lane down which he was advancing, for what was beneath him was fine gravel, evenly raked. And of course the trees, too, were now explained. He had turned off along something quite different from what he had supposed; he was on a well-tended avenue leading to some private house. Unless, indeed, 'inn' on the map meant nothing of the kind, but some more pretentious establishment of the kind nowadays known as a country-house hotel.

Such a place would at least be bound to offer some sort of hospitality. Appleby moved on, and almost at once sensed that he was heading for an even deeper opacity than that which had hitherto surrounded him. Deep and *large*. A great rectangular block of blackness, which for a moment he thought to interpret as an enormous barn. And then, in another moment, the scene (if it could be called that) was shatteringly transformed. In place of blinding obscurity there was equally blinding light. For seconds Appleby's night-attuned vision was utterly confounded. Then he saw that what had sprung into existence before him was an imposing mansion-house. Its every window was uncurtained – and all had been simultaneously illuminated. The effect was as of a great fanfare of trumpets released upon the dark.

Chapter Two

This confusion of the senses – which the learned would have described as a synaesthesia – lasted only for a moment; but Appleby's mere bewilderment didn't so quickly abate. For time, too, was playing a trick upon him. He might have been Proust's Marcel, hard upon imbibing the displeasing little sopped *madeleine* which brought his childhood flooding back to memory. Appleby was a small provincial boy again; and there had arrived the grand climax of the Christmas holidays. The Cave of the Demon King – a murky place at best – had vanished momentarily into entire darkness, and had been succeeded in a flash by the dazzling and breath-taking splendours of the Palace of the Fairy Prince. The 'transformation scene' of the pantomime had begun.

The anachronistic promise did not, of course, fulfil itself. The massive Palladian façade before which he stood at gaze showed no sign of twitching, quivering, revolving, lifting, parting in order to reveal those farther and interior splendours amid which the entire company would presently assemble to receive the just plaudits of the audience. Appleby's surprising encounter was with quite solid stone and mortar.

He stepped quickly behind a tree. This might have been judged an odd reaction on the part of a respectable citizen to the sudden appearance before him of an even more respectable house. But old-established professional habit was at work;

11

he had often enough found swift evasive movement to be healthy when something abruptly enigmatic occurred. The mysterious, moreover, was apt to associate itself in his mind with crime, whether achieved or designed; and it was because of this that his thought now took the turn it did. What confronted him, he conjectured, might be a species of eccentric but effective burglar alarm. Unauthorized nocturnal intrusion within the purlieus of this august habitation automatically produced not a ringing of bells or the like, but a deluge of light calculated to appal and repel even the most temerarious burglar. The measure was certainly an extravagant one, and there seemed an unnerving possibility that the mind devising it might have backed it up with others more positively disagreeable. The landed gentry of England – not to speak of the great territorial aristocracy – harboured a good many individuals inclined to linger behind the times. The trend of modern social legislation being disposed to develop on somewhat democratic and even egalitarian lines, the employment of man-traps and spring-guns designed to ensure that an Englishman's castle should *be* his castle had undoubtedly fallen largely into desuetude. But here and there squirarchal persons disposed to walk in the ancient ways might be continuing to direct such engines upon intruders disposed to walk where they shouldn't. Alternatively – and more prosaically – a dangerously excited proprietor, or even butler, might at any moment emerge from the alerted house with a loaded shot-gun. It was with appropriate caution that Appleby peered out from his shelter now.

The house perched, as such places do, upon a basement storey out of which alone a good many reasonably commodious dwellings might have been carved. There was a dominating central block with a Corinthian portico, and on each side of this quadrant corridors connected with substantial and symmetrical wings. It seemed probable that the same effect was repeated at the back – in which case what one would view from the air would be something like a giant crab or sprawled four-footed beast. The whole pile wasn't all that vast; one might have called it – Appleby reflected – a Kedleston Hall cunningly miniaturized; but it was undeniably imposing, all the same. Whatever its present economic hinterland, it had been built

12

for somebody who knew himself to be the person of principal consequence for a great many miles around. And here it was, consuming electricity at a prodigious rate for reasons which remained decidedly unclear.

For the burglar-alarm theory didn't at all explain all those uncurtained windows. The effect of sudden pervasive illumination would be quite adequately startling even through drawn curtains or lowered blinds, and that the whole mansion should be condemned to a kind of lidless vigil in order to produce a marginally more striking impact upon some hypothetical housebreaker made no sense at all. So Appleby tried another guess. Might the place be both untenanted and disfurnished – a mere empty shell in which some defective master-switch or the like intermittently produced this weird manifestation? Electrical contrivances did, after all, behave badly at times. His own torch had done so, only half an hour ago.

This seemed excessively improbable, too. And certainly the house was not abandoned. The light pouring from it illuminated everything immediately round about, and the resulting suggestion was of a property in apple-pie order. The windows, moreover, could be distinguished as not mere bleak rectangles; one could discern the silhouette of curtains formally drawn back, blinds lowered by the prescriptive few inches of daytime use, and here and there what might be the looking-glass on a dressing-table. In one wing, furthermore, the ground-floor windows came down to the level of the terrace upon which they gave; and through these it was possible for Appleby to view the book-lined walls of a library.

His gaze travelled up to the roof. He was too close to the house to command anything here except a long bold cornice and a crowning balustrade. Behind this there possibly lurked lines of attic windows. No chimneys were visible. But when he raised a hand to shade his eyes from the main glare he could just detect against the dark sky beyond a single faint column of smoke. For a moment he wondered whether the place was on fire. If the house was closed and untenanted, and a fire had broken out through some faulty electrical installation, it was conceivable that the untoward spectacle to which he was being treated was in some way a result.

13

But this – Appleby told himself impatiently – really made no more sense than anything else that had so far come into his head. It required one to believe that the lights throughout the house had been turned on severally, that all had then been simultaneously extinguished at a main switch, and that now some accident had reversed the process. This just wouldn't do. The spectacle before him was a spectacle deliberately contrived.

Having arrived at this conclusion, Appleby decided he must investigate. Investigation had been his *métier*, after all.

It would not have occurred to him to ascribe to himself anything that could be called a fanciful mind. But imagination of a sort had been pretty regularly required of him, and it sometimes took odd turns. This happened now. The house *was* like a giant crab – one out of some sort of old-fashioned science fiction and to be thought of, perhaps, as madly luminous on the bed of ocean. The curving corridors, each connecting with a wing fully twenty yards in front of the main building, were preparing to exercise a pincer movement on him at any moment. They would grab, and then the whole phosphorescent enormity would execute a rapid sideways retreat into a vast subaqueous cavern.

In spite of this alarming notion, Appleby walked straight up to the house. Or rather he walked straight to the foot of the impressive flight of steps – a to-and-fro affair lavishly provided with balustrades, urns and statuary – which would elevate him to the base of the main portico and presumably enable him to present himself before the principal door of the mansion. It wasn't quite evident what he ought then to do. Simply ring a bell, perhaps, and see what happened. Appleby had a vision of a stately man-servant answering his summons, and receiving not too well anything that he could find in his head to say. But he would be perfectly justified, after all, in representing himself as a distressed wayfarer in need of succour. Perhaps he ought to have brought that useless gear-lever with him. It would, in a fashion, have attested his *bona fides*.

He had climbed the last steps, and was beneath the lofty portico. It was only dimly lit. He walked towards its centre, and turned to face the house. At last its front door was before him. It was a suitably impressive double-leaved affair. And it was wide open.

Inside was a warm glow – warm, although the effect that the revealed décor suggested ought surely to have been decidedly chilly. For here was a hall which was certainly the height of the whole building, with colonnades of alabaster Corinthian columns and a coved ceiling in the Adam style. The general impression was of a great deal of marble and quite a lot of gold. But most of the light was reflected from areas of the ceiling which were predominantly in Italian pink. It was this that lent a certain august cosiness – almost a welcoming quality – to the scene of which Appleby thus found himself to be enjoying a totally unexpected view.

The autumn night, although it couldn't be called chilly, was far from warm, and it could not conceivably be to admit the air that the door before him stood wide open as it did. But nobody was coming out – nor, equally clearly, had anybody just gone in. Nor again, in the great void hall was anybody in view. Beyond the long expanse of marble floor, boldly figured as in some classical basilica, the columned vista closed upon lofty doors which no doubt admitted to the domed saloon upon which the whole house must pivot. But of living things there wasn't so much as a domestic cat. Nor did the most muted sound of any sort float to Appleby's ear.

But at least there was a perfectly ordinary door-bell. He put out a hand and rang. There was nothing wrong with the bell, for he could just hear its summons in some distant and probable subterraneous place. He waited. It would only be reasonable to wait for quite some time. But nothing happened. He rang again.

A long silence. Appleby realized that a fresh problem confronted him. Before this unaccountable and even slightly unnerving state of affairs, he supposed, it would be irresponsible simply to turn and walk away. Nor did the prospect of continued blind wandering through the small hours appeal to him in the least. Servants ought to appear. The servants ought to be followed by the owner of the property, who would presently be unobtrusively anxious to provide the hospitality

15

which, in such circumstances, one gentleman owes to another. There would be drinks, a common acquaintance or two would be discovered; after a little civil talk, Appleby would be shown to a comfortable bed.

But this wasn't happening. And in front of him was this open door, this opulent and seemingly unprotected mansion. Action of some sort was incumbent upon him. Perhaps the proper initial step was to circumambulate the exterior of the whole house, seeking somewhere in its obscurer offices a lurking caretaker who might explain the mystery. But he didn't really think much of this. He was a Justice of the Peace, and the Queen's commission ought surely to justify a little mild trespass in face of the untoward circumstances confronting him. Appleby walked through the open door.

He had an instant sense of being observed. So strong was this that he halted at once, and in a voice not pitched above that of normal conversation asked: 'Is there anybody at home here?' Only a faint echo answered him. But in a colonnaded chamber like this as many people as there were columns could play at a kind of hide-and-seek. He took a couple of paces forward, and glanced between the first two pale honey-coloured shafts. He was indeed being observed, and in a further moment he saw that it was by a whole company. Sightlessly, however, and by a double row of marble statues set in niches in either wall. They were an incongruous assemblage of undraped Greek divinities and of English gentlemen – some in huge tie wigs and some in hunting perukes. It seemed improbable that any information could be extracted from them – except, indeed, that they further attested to the general consequence of their invisible owner.

There was at least nothing much – Appleby noted with professional approval – that a nefariously disposed person could walk away with. Anything that could be called furniture in this vast space was confined to marble benches and elaborately inlaid marble tables for which substantial machinery would be required if they were to be budged an inch. Appleby walked the full length of the hall, and opened the door at the end. The saloon – a square chamber rendered semi-octagonal by the presence of large statue-filled niches in each corner – was in much the same formally bleak condition, except that here the benches and tables (which he guessed to be Spanish) were in ancient wood, and were disposed on and around a Persian carpet which was certainly beautiful and probably very valuable indeed. Appleby surveyed this, frowning. He turned back, found another door, and opened it upon what proved to be a drawing-room. There was only a low light here, but it was quite good enough to reveal a pilferer's paradise. Within fragile cabinets, or disposed upon the finely polished surface of sundry tables and escritoires, were innumerable objects of virtu – good, bad and largely indifferent – of the sort that silt up over the generations in a house of this kind. But Appleby's eye didn't linger on these; it had been attracted to a painting over the mantelshelf. He crossed the room and studied this with attention. He was left in very little doubt that the painter had been Claude. It was decidedly not the sort of possession that ought to be left hanging around.

Newspapers and magazines, of course, were another matter. There would be no great disaster in some dishonest person's making off with *The Times*, the *Field*, or *Country Life* ... Appleby found that he had paused before a neatly ordered pile of these. He picked up a daily paper. It bore the date of the previous day.

And now a satisfactory idea came to Appleby at last. There was nothing unique about this place. Several score of such lay scattered about England. Unlived in, but given a contrary appearance for the better satisfaction of the curious, they were open daily to anybody who cared to pay half-a-crown at the door. There wouldn't even be a former owner lurking in a private wing, as was the case in many houses of the kind. Ownership was vested in some trust or society dedicated to thus preserving the tokens of what was popularly (and erroneously) regarded as a vanished way of life. It would all be very well done. Fresh flowers would appear daily, there would be linen on the beds, the dining-room would be set out as for a modest banquet for some thirty persons.

But here, of course, was only the first part of the explanation Appleby had hit upon. Yet the rest was easy. There had been a failure in the electrical system; it was being repaired and

17

tested over-night so as not to interfere with the normal museum-like routine of the mansion; and the workmen engaged on the job were being disgracefully regardless of the elementary considerations of security.

Appleby was much astonished that all this hadn't come to him at once.

But he had to decide what to do in the light of his discovery. His own position was more than a little odd. A landed proprietor was one thing; he would recognize, so to speak, the smell of Appleby's tweeds. But a crowd of electricians might well take him for a cunning crook talking posh. It would be prudent not to give the appearance of having been detected by them, but rather himself to act in a decisive way at the start. Having formed this wise resolve, Appleby returned to the hall, and this time addressed the empty air from fully expanded lungs. 'Is there anybody around?' he shouted – and was astonished and gratified by the racket he thus produced. The sound-waves positively bounced about the marble walls and alabaster columns like a ball on a pin-table. But the uproar died away without effect. None replied. Only Appleby had the impression that one of the staring gentlemen in wigs had assumed a stony expression (in every sense), as if deprecating so vulgar and gross an outcry.

He had, of course, misjudged the dimensions of the place. That was it. The workmen were in some corner of it too remote for hearing. Indeed, supplying the load of electricity which might be consumed by so large a house probably needed an installation so substantial as to occupy a small building of its own. His only course was to explore further. This time, he left the hall on the side opposite the drawing-room, and found himself confronted by the principal staircase of the house. It was a wooden staircase, light and graceful except for stout newels, and with consoled step-ends delicately carved. Robert Adam's own, Appleby told himself – and reflected, fleetingly and learnedly, that he would bet a dozen bottles of claret on the house-architects having been the elder Brettingham and the younger Paine. But for this kind of leisured connoisseurship (for which he had rather a weakness) the time was not apposite. He skirted the staircase, which there seemed no call to ascend, and tried another door. It took him into a large bed-room.

There was nothing surprising in this. It had been a Georgian habit to have a single master-bedroom, together with certain ancillary chambers, on the principal floor. And here they were. As he had foretold, there was a fully made-up bed on view. It was even turned down, and a pair of men's silk pyjamas were laid out upon it. Appleby felt this to be going a bit far. The effect was as of the service of the dead as it is found in certain Egyptian tombs. Less exotically, it was rather as Queen Victoria had insisted on things being ordered and disposed for the personal comfort of her deceased Consort. Only for Prince Albert, Appleby supposed, it would have been not pyjamas but a night-gown and nightcap ... Appleby found that he was looking no longer at the pyjamas but at the centre of the lower half of the bed. Surely that small hump just distinguish-able beneath the eiderdown quilt could speak of only one thing? Swiftly – but not without a childishly apprehensive glance over his shoulder – Appleby thrust a hand within the sheets. There was not a doubt about what it encountered. It was a hot-water bottle. And the hot-water bottle was *hot*.

This time Sir John Appleby (J.P., and lately retired from the position of Commissioner of Metropolitan Police) was really shaken. What could have persuaded him – just because he had fondly supposed there to be something *odd* about this house – thus to barge in upon the bed-chamber of what appeared to be a single gentleman obviously moving in the upper reaches of society? Appleby felt rather like Goldilocks when she began to apprehend the possible arrival of the Three Bears.

He retreated hastily, and with a distinct sense that he had better begin to *think*. Ever since his car came unstuck, he had been doing little more than doze comfortably along. There is something relaxing in a crisis that one knows perfectly well to be no crisis at all; in a minute disturbance of expectation or routine which will certainly do no more than keep one an un-wonted two or three hours out of bed. But he wasn't too sure now that he hadn't stumbled upon something of a different order. And he didn't really and truly believe that it was either a bears' den or a mare's nest.

Chapter Three

Next to the big bedroom was the dining-room – although some small connecting apartment had been converted into a bathroom and corridor in recent years. Here, too, was a very rational eighteenth-century disposition of things. The footmen, one supposed, had only this short distance to transport their master at the conclusion of the evening's convivialities. Equally, the transit would be feasible, in a hobbling way, during an otherwise incapacitating attack of gout. But Appleby was less struck by these considerations than by the spectacle the room presented to his view. The dining-table, although it had been abbreviated to its minimum number of leaves, was still very large and long. And – again as he had predicted – it had been set out for a meal. Only – and quite contrary to his expectation – it was a meal for a single person. And a *real* meal.

Quite a simple real meal. The silver and the crystal were there, but it was their quality and not their quantity that might impress. Six candles – and they hadn't been burning long. A decanter of what might be madeira, with an appropriate glass. One other glass, for champagne. And – iced in a bucket – a bottle of champagne. There was cold food on a side-table. There were covered dishes on the electric hot-plate. Momentarily, Appleby had to resist the conclusion that this feast had been set out for *him*. Then he remembered how Goldilocks had sat down to the porridge.

But *somebody* was expected. Of this there could be no doubt at all. And – once more – it might all be very simple. The person entitled to sup in this way was expected to arrive very late, or rather very early. The servants had been instructed not to wait up. They had simply retired to bed in some distant region appropriate to their quality.

This all made sense – if somewhat eccentric sense. But not that open front door. The Claude, and much else, might by now have been fifty miles away in a burglarious van or pantechnicon. Even if an employer had given so absurd an instruction, no responsible servant in such an establishment would have done more than pretend to concur with it, and somebody would have been set to keep an eye on things in a quiet way. Already, in fact, Appleby would have been embarrassingly apprehended. The whole thing remained an enigma still.

Appleby considered finding a telephone and calling the local police. They would at least tell him where he was. But then – having received so strange a report or enquiry – they would themselves arrive in no time, and the resulting situation would be awkward and absurd. Perhaps he could ring the telephone exchange, announce that he had suddenly lost his memory, and demand to know not only *where* he was but *who* he was. But this idea was merely frivolous. He dismissed, at least for the time being, any notion of having recourse to the telephone.

But there must be other means of discovering at least some relevant information about this dispeopled, yet mysteriously waiting and expectant house. He remembered the library he had seen through french windows from the drive, and it struck him as a likely source of knowledge. That had been in one of the wings – the one on the drawing-room side. He would find, and make his way down, the quadrant corridor leading to it. In a house like this it would probably be known as the private wing, and that on the dining-room side would be the kitchen wing, which was quite likely to contain servants' quarters also. It might be as well to make his way there first, and do a little more shouting.

The first of these expeditions – kitchenwards – was entirely negative in its results – except, indeed, that a large number of small empty rooms on an upper storey presented a puzzling suggestion of the present non-existence of any domestic staff at all. But the library was more interesting. It proved to be a room of moderate size, furnished for comfort rather than ostentation. The impression was enhanced by the fact that, behind a large glass screen, a bright wood fire was burning on the hearth.

These appearances were ceasing to be surprising, and Appleby merely reflected that here was the source of that column of smoke. What was much more significant for his present purpose was a large eighteenth-century topographical engraving hanging above the fireplace. It represented, without a doubt, the building in which he now stood. He walked over to it, and found that it bore an inscription in flowing and much-embellished copperplate. This read:

Ledward Park
The seat of Augustus Snodgrass Esquire

Although somewhat surprised, Appleby reflected that an Augustus Snodgrass had a perfect right to existence outside the covers of *Pickwick Papers*. Perhaps Dickens had borrowed the name from a family tomb in the neighbouring parish church. The name Snodgrass, indeed, suggested itself as having been that of a citizen rather than a member of the ancient nobility of the realm. But plenty of eighteenth-century city men had bought or built themselves houses quite as grand as Ledward Park. Appleby hoped that the family still flourished, and that he would make the acquaintance of some member of it soon. He was beginning to feel that he was spending altogether too lonely a night. But perhaps he could gather a little more information first.

There was a desk in one of the windows; but it was unpromisingly bare. Besides, he could hardly start rummaging in private papers. But works of reference were another matter. *Who's Who* might turn up a relevant Snodgrass or two, and on Ledward as a property the invaluable *Landed Gentry* ought to help. These should certainly be in this room. For that matter, there was still something relevant in his own pocket. He could take another look at his map.

He did so, spreading out the sheet on the desk beside him. And there, at least, Ledward Park was. The house, plus an actual park, was given some prominence, but the avenue was only faintly indicated, which must be why he had missed it in the first place. He looked at it now with a not very logical sense of its giving him some assurance that this entire adventure wasn't a dream. And then he made a further inspection of the library. On three of its walls the books went up to the ceiling, so that the upper rows could be reached, or even identified, only from a library-ladder. There must be seven or eight thousand volumes, Appleby supposed, but he doubted whether the collection was particularly valuable. It looked like the typical country-house miscellaneous affair, with here and there coherent patches which suggested some vein of scholarship uncertainly surfacing in the family from time to time. There was a respectable assemblage of *Antarctica*, and one entire bay was devoted to the history and geography of South America. What was called standard literature wasn't much in evidence, and Appleby didn't notice a single work of fiction. It seemed almost possible to believe that the Snodgrasses of Ledward Park had remained ignorant of the existence of their poetically disposed Dickensian namesake.

The fourth wall was given over – and perhaps it might be informatively – to family portraits of the minor order: oil sketches, pastels, miniatures, pencil drawings, and photographs both ancient and modern. There was a handsome Victorian gentleman drawn by Richmond – a distinguished performance contrasting oddly with the stiffly posed, although technically accomplished 'studies' by Victorian and Edwardian cameras. In these, generously bosomed but decently swathed ladies inclined their noses demonstratively over vases of flowers; gentlemen eased the unwonted process of absorbing themselves in a book by leaning a thoughtful brow on a supporting hand; children strangled kittens, clasped hoops, or with outstretched battledore unconvincingly simulated the expectation of a shuttlecock's arriving thereupon. One small boy attracted Appleby's notice. He had 'dressed up' in military uniform – not the unassuming cardboard 'outfit' Appleby remembered from his own childhood, but in well-tailored garments suggestive of some foreign, rather than a British, regiment. The boy had been firmly positioned four-square before the camera – his left arm stiffly at attention; his right hand also at his side, resting in an officer-like fashion on the hilt of his miniature sword; his eyes steadily fixed upon the threatening lens. Thus dragooned, the small boy nevertheless contrived to intimate in some indefinable way the possession of an unruly spirit. Appleby wondered whether a real army had eventually claimed him; and, if so, what it had made of him. Perhaps a battlefield had claimed him – in Burma, the Western Desert,

Normandy. At a guess, he had been of about the right age for that.

The little portrait gallery – the unassuming domestic note of which struck Appleby as rather pleasing in the middle of this grand house – was disappointing as a source of information. Nothing exhibited either a name or a date, so he was no further forward in discovering whether Snodgrasses still inhabited (or ought to be inhabiting) Ledward Park. He fell back on his former plan, and hunted around for *Who's Who*. It proved not difficult to run to earth, and in its pages several Snodgrasses revealed themselves at once. The very first entry, moreover, appeared to be the one he sought. Adrian Snodgrass, described in the opening line of the notice as 'soldier and traveller', had been born in 1915, the second and now eldest surviving son of a brigadier. He was unmarried. His schooling had been partly in Azuera, South America, and partly at Harrow. He had gone to Oxford, entered a good regiment, resigned his commission within a couple of years, turned up in another South American country as a military attaché in the British Embassy, quitted this apparently in the interest of 'exploration', been later 'associated with various governmental agencies' in Azuera, and then shifted his activities to Africa. He had published a book unendearingly entitled *My Niger Niggers*, after – and perhaps because of – which he had returned to Azuera and been 'prominent in securing measures of political reform'. With this activity, ascribed to 1961, the record ended. Adrian Snodgrass's address was given as care of Professor Beddoes Snodgrass, Ledward Park.

This further Snodgrass appeared – several Snodgrasses on – on the opposite page. Beddoes, who was a widower in his seventies and apparently a younger brother of the brigadier, was also a soldier, and indeed the son of a soldier. He had seen active service, taught at the Staff College, left the army to lecture on military history at universities in South America, and eventually become Professor of the History of Warfare at Cambridge. His publications had not been numerous; what seemed to be the most important of them was called *Terrain and Tactics: Three Campaigns in Brazil*. His address was The Old Dower House, Ledward.

Having provided himself with this succinctly rendered information, Appleby proceeded to digest it as well as he could. For this purpose he established himself in a comfortable chair before the fire. This was no doubt a further stage in the mild impropriety of his conduct. But it was going to be his attitude, he told himself, that he had stood in as caretaker of Ledward until a better turned up.

It was a fair inference from the record, he supposed, that the owner of the house was Adrian Snodgrass, who had followed the military tradition of his family, left the army for what suggested itself as having been a wandering and adventurous life, and seen no reason to provide the world with any information about his activities for a period of what was now more than ten years. He might be dead – but, if so, it was unlikely that he had been dead for long: otherwise, *Who Was Who* would be the volume in which his career was chronicled. What else could be inferred about this descendant – as he presumably was – of Augustus Snodgrass Esquire? He didn't announce himself as having a club, and a London club was a convenience which it would occur to few Englishmen of some substance and of nomadic habit to do without. It was conceivable that the missing latter part of Adrian's life had landed him in some situation incompatible with continued membership of anything of the sort. This might be so without its following that he was a thoroughly bad hat. There were all sorts of possibilities upon which it was idle to speculate.

As this went through his mind, Appleby found that he had turned in his chair to take another look at the small boy in the soldier's uniform. He had a hunch that this was Adrian. In which case the uniform was perhaps a replica of something South American. It was clear from the record that Adrian had spent at least some active years in South America. And this, taken in conjunction with the other *Who's Who* entry, suggested that the Snodgrasses were one of those English families which had for some generations maintained contact with relations settled in one or another of the South American states.

Appleby turned to review the other little life-story he had paused upon. Beddoes Snodgrass was Adrian's uncle, and he too had been a soldier. But he had exchanged, as Shakespeare put it, the casque for the cushion, and there was every appearance of his having enjoyed a blameless and useful academic career. His book on Brazil was no doubt a standard work. He now appeared to live in retirement on the Ledward estate. The Old Dower House might be a couple of miles away, or it might be no more than a hundred yards. And Adrian's address was given as care of Professor Snodgrass at Ledward Park itself. It looked as if this elderly character managed his nephew's house and affairs. At the moment, he seemed not to be looking after them too well.

It was at this moment that Appleby heard voices.

He stood up and faced the door, prepared to explain himself. For here, surely, was Beddoes Snodgrass after all. If, as was popularly believed, all professors were absent-minded, then perhaps emeritus professors were liable to an intensification of this condition amounting to intermittent amnesia. Beddoes Snodgrass had been working late in this empty house; he had possibly intended to sleep here; and his own servants had been instructed to prepare a meal and withdraw to the Old Dower House. Later, Snodgrass had obliviously tottered home, gone to bed, and then awakened to the memory that he had neither eaten his dinner, turned out his eccentric blaze of lights, or so much as shut the front door. So here he was back again, accompanied by a retainer who had guided his aged footsteps through the night.

This would have been an excellent explanation – quite the best and simplest Appleby had thought up yet – but for the fact that his ear had briefly betrayed him. The voices weren't coming from the quadrant-corridor. They were coming from outside the house.

Appleby's hypothesis, of course, still didn't need to be abandoned. The learned Snodgrass was at hand, but still only traversing the terrace outside this part of the private wing. Yet there was surely something a little odd . . . Appleby strode rapidly to one of the uncurtained windows. For what he had heard couldn't be described as conversation. It was much more like a hoarse whispering. And he had no sooner realized this than there came a sudden clatter as of some small metal object dropped on flags. There followed a muttered curse, and the sound of several pairs of rapidly retreating footsteps. By the time Appleby got the french window open silence had returned. And nowhere within the glow radiating from the house was the slightest movement to be seen.

Appleby shut the window again, and turned back into the room. It was to find that he was no longer alone, for in the doorway of the library stood a very old man.

'You've aged a great deal,' the very old man said.

Chapter Four

'Professor Snodgrass?' Appleby began. 'I owe you . . .'

'But your eyes haven't changed.' Professor Snodgrass (who got along on a stick with a thick rubber tip) had taken a few steps forward, and was glancing at the photograph of the boy-soldier. 'No, not since you were a child. Nor your nature either, I suppose.' The Professor produced a chuckle which appeared to betoken indulgence rather than censure. 'At least you keep your word – eh?'

'My dear sir, you are quite mistaken. My name . . .'

'Later than you might have done. But let that be, my dear boy. I have kept my word too. It's one of our few family virtues, as your dear father used to say. The candle in the window, and the table spread. Have you had your supper yet?'

'Professor Snodgrass, I am very sorry – but I have occasioned a total misapprehension. You are supposing me to be a relation, whereas I am an entire stranger. My name is Appleby, and I have no business at Ledward at all.'

'No more you have. What a deuced odd thing!' The Professor took out a watch and consulted it. 'But the night remains young, and Adrian may turn up still. Did you say you were a friend of his? He has made an appointment with you?'

'Nothing of the sort.' The awkwardness of the occasion, Appleby reflected, was being enhanced by the fact that this aged academic person was no longer very fully in command of his wits. 'It is simply that my car broke down a couple of miles away . . .'

'That's very bad – very bad, indeed.' The Professor was suddenly emphatic. 'Reliable transport, I have always insisted, is the vital condition of success in the field. Firepower itself comes second to it. And my own vote is for camels, every time. I am delighted that you are interested in the subject. You and I must have a talk about the Sudan. I have been doing a good deal of work lately on the Juba River expedition of 1875. By the way, have you ever asked yourself why it took Sir Samuel Baker all that time to reach Gondokoro in 1870? We must take a careful look at the maps. Only tonight I am a little preoccupied by the arrival of my nephew Adrian Snodgrass, whom you no doubt know. Have the servants shown you to your room?'

'No. You see . . .'

'Ah, that is because there *are* no servants. Not here at the Park. My own people just come over, you see, from time to time.' Professor Snodgrass paused, rather as if some perplexing problem had suddenly presented itself to him. And then his brow cleared. 'And so do I,' he said. 'That accounts for my being here now.' He fleetingly looked with great acuteness at Appleby. 'But it doesn't account for *your* being here. I'm far from certain there isn't something damned fishy about you. I think perhaps I'd better call the police.'

'By all means do. It's an excellent idea. They will quite quickly be able to reassure you about me, as a matter of fact. Which won't mean that I shan't still owe you a great many apologies.'

'My dear fellow, nothing of the kind is needed – nothing at all.' The inconsequence of Professor Snodgrass seemed capable of continuing indefinitely and, as it were, *accelerando*. 'May I suggest our taking a glass of wine while waiting for my nephew? Working over here from time to time as I do, I have them keep a decanter of port in that little cupboard by the desk. Quinta do Noval '55, at the moment. Modest but wholesome stuff. To put my lips to when I am so dispoged. Are you a Dickensian? The great novelist honoured my family, it may be said, quite early in his career.' Not waiting for a reply,

Appleby's host (as he might now be called) made his way almost briskly to the cupboard he had indicated, and did in fact produce from it a decanter and two glasses. He set them on a table, and courteously motioned Appleby to a chair. 'Delightful of you to have dropped in,' he said. 'I am conscious of seeing too little of my neighbours nowadays.'

Although no more a neighbour than a nephew, Appleby drank his port with a clear conscience. He had done his best to clarify the anomalous position in which he found himself. He was inclined to wonder – although he couldn't quite have told why – whether Beddoes Snodgrass was altogether as crazed as he seemed. The old man's words, like Hamlet's, were wild and whirling. But his glance, at least intermittently, was that of one who knew a hawk from a handsaw. And no doubt a steady assumption of his rationality was the best means of getting a modicum of sense out of him. Although curious, Appleby acknowledged to himself that the why and wherefore of Adrian Snodgrass's being expected to turn up at Ledward in the watches of the night was no business of his. But what he had heard on the terrace was another matter. It had rendered the effect, indeed, of amateur effort. But it certainly hadn't been effort in any lawful direction. It would be irresponsible not to try to bring this old creature to some sense of the hazard to which his eccentric proceedings were putting his property – or his missing nephew's property. Appleby decided to tackle this head-on.

'Professor Snodgrass,' he said, 'I have something to urge upon you. And it is relevant to begin by saying that I am a retired policeman.'

'India, eh?' The Professor appeared much interested. 'Very decent service, to my mind. Never been adequately recognized. I expect you knew my friend Strickland. Ran your show on the hush-hush side. Keeping an eye on the Tsar, and all that.'

'Not India. London.'

'Oh.' Professor Snodgrass's interest sensibly diminished. But then he suddenly set down his glass. 'Didn't you say Appleby? It's not Sir John Appleby?'

'Yes, it is.'

'Dear me!' The Professor appeared to recognize that he had occasioned surprise by being thus swiftly on the ball. 'Odd thing – but I remember Tommy Titherton used to talk about you. When he was Home Secretary, that was. I'm delighted to have you call. Curious that I should have taken you for Adrian. He'll be amused to hear about it. I expect him at any moment.'

'I shall be interested to meet him.' Appleby found this futher example of matter and impertinency mixed no less baffling than before. 'But my point is that, just as a point of professional feeling, I don't like coming across open invitations to crime. And that's what your open house it. A very open invitation to crime indeed. I've seen that the Park is full of valuable things – and I've done so while roaming in without anybody to stop me.'

'Ah, but you forget the candle in the window.'

'I beg your pardon?'

'One of my promises to Adrian. I interpret it a shade liberally, my dear Sir John, by flicking a switch that turns on every light in Ledward.'

'I'm very aware of the resulting effect.'

'No doubt – or no doubt in one sense. But have you considered how it must take burglars, and fellows of that sort? Scare them out of their wits, my dear chap.'

'Once in a way – perhaps.' Appleby paused. 'I don't want to be intrusive, but may I know how often you – well, mount this ritual reception for your nephew? It's not every night of the week?'

'Heavens above, no!' Professor Snodgrass's astonishment sounded entirely sane. 'Only on Adrian's birthday, of course. That was our compact, you know.'

'Very well. But surely it must be known for miles around that this extraordinary affair happens yearly: Ledward all prepared for the return of its owner (as I suppose your nephew to be) and then vacated?'

'Known for miles around?' Professor Snodgrass had the air of one confronting a novel idea. 'But what if it is? Over that sort of area they're all our own people, more or less. They'd be as delighted to see Adrian back as I'd be.'

'No doubt.' Appleby judged it pointless to question this squirearchal assumption. 'But, you know, quite apart from this annual tryst you keep, the house strikes me as uncommonly vulnerable to burglary. If, that is, it is regularly untenanted by night – which is what I seem to gather from you. May I ask if the Dower House is far away?'

'The Old Dower House. The New Dower House is a ruin. I'm just across the park. Matter of less than half a mile. Fellow from the insurance company did once come and take up your point. Had a lot to say about rascals who steal pictures, and so forth. Of course I reassured him. Showed him my double action Colt. Reliable weapon. Used by an uncle of mine, as a matter of fact, at Balaclava.'

Appleby again had his moment of suspicion about Professor Snodgrass. Had it been wholly fanciful to imagine a slight pause before the word 'Balaclava', as if his host had been considering saying 'Waterloo' instead?

'Mark you, we have had one alarm.' Snodgrass was at his most reasonable again. 'It was only last year, as a matter of fact.'

'You mean on this particular night last year?'

'Of course – on Adrian's birthday. I came over to the Park to see if he had turned up. As a matter of fact, he hadn't, and I decided to wait for a while. Not here, come to think of it, but in the drawing-room. I was on the *qui vive*, you know. Odd expression that. It means *Long live who?* Same sort of challenge as *Under which king, Bezonian? speak, or die!* Are you a Shakespeare man? I've always been a strong Shakespeare man myself. Used to have long chats about the plays with Mr Kipling. Another strong Shakespeare man. Bible too. Amazing.'

'And what was the result of your being on the *qui vive*?'

'I heard these noises outside. Thought it was opossums.'

'Opossums?'

'Yes – but the Australian kind. Got to know them when I did an A.D.C. spell there as a young man. Climb on the roof or under it, or fool around on your verandah. Cough and wheeze

31

and jibber so that you'd swear it was half a regiment of senile tramps.'

'You thought you heard half a regiment of senile tramps outside your drawing-room?'

'Well, approximately that. Just some fellows up to no good. Proposing to break and enter, eh? But they cleared out when I shouted at them.'

'I see. But I suppose they could have entered *without* breaking? Walked in, I mean, through your symbolically open door, just as I've done tonight.'

'I'm very sorry there was nobody to receive you, my dear Appleby.' The Professor's port appeared to be prompting its proprietor to cordiality. 'Must have appeared uncommonly uncivil. But it just so happens, you see, that you've turned up on rather an exceptional night.'

'I've tumbled to that.'

'Nothing of the kind. I've been most uncommunicative. Another uncivil thing. Very conscious that I owe you an explanation. So I'm going to tell you about Adrian.'

It is a principle of the human mind that information which it may be *intriguant* to ferret out for oneself becomes potentially boring as soon as it is volunteered by somebody else. And this principle obtains with particular force in the minds of retired professional detectives. Appleby in his retirement found himself at times positively prowling round for some small mystery to bite on; conversely, being addressed in an instructive way by other people frequently prompted him (as it did Dr Johnson) to remove his mind and think of Tom Thumb. So he was suddenly not at all sure that he wanted to hear the life-story of Adrian Snodgrass. The mild duty he had felt to protect property wantonly exposed to larceny had lured him into and around Ledward, and the sounds he had heard outside the library disposed him to believe that his solicitude had been by no means idle. But in the face of Professor Snodgrass's regardlessness in the matter there seemed to be little more he could do. And as for Adrian (Appleby suspected), the more one heard about him, the less was one likely to be charmed or edified. He bore all the signs of belonging to that sizeable flock of black sheep which the English upper classes, collectively regarded, are concerned to maintain at pasture in regions of the globe as remote as possible. Adrian Snodgrass was perhaps peculiar in that he possessed, in the Ledward estate, a tolerably rich home pasture which he didn't appear much to bother about – and in that he possessed, too, in the form of an aged military historian, a doating relative who yearly made bizarre and elaborate preparations for a return to the fold which, in all probability, was never going to happen. And if it *did* happen – if by any conceivable chance the long-lost heir turned up this very night – the occasion would not be one at which a total stranger could with any propriety assist.

Nevertheless Appleby was fairly caught. He could not now with civility rise to his feet and offer brief farewells. And the Professor, he noticed, had poured another glass of port for each of them. If he had kept his vigil in solitude for years – as was rather to be supposed – he was far from disconcerted at having a companion on this occasion. In fact, he was enjoying it. Simple humanity required Appleby to sit back and listen.

'As a young man, or indeed as a boy,' Professor Snodgrass began, 'Adrian was remarkable for ...' He broke off. 'My dear Appleby,' he said, 'have you heard anything?'

It must certainly have been true that Appleby *looked* as if he were hearing something. His sitting back had abruptly become a sitting forward as if at the bidding of an alerted sense. He had turned, moreover, to look at the french window which he had shut again after his recent survey of the terrace beyond it. The window was shut still.

'Heard anything?' Appleby repeated. 'Well, no. But what about smell? Do you smell anything out of the way?'

'I can't say that I do.' The Professor was reasonably surprised. 'A whiff of stale tobacco, perhaps? I smoke a cigar in this room from time to time. Delighted to find you one now. Neglectful of me.'

'Not tobacco. I'd be inclined to say Chanel.'

'Camel?' Appleby's host seemed gratified rather than puzzled. 'You must be right. Not a thing it's easy to mistake, eh?

Adrian arrived on one, no doubt. Capital means of transport, as I think I said.'

But Appleby had jumped to his feet, and was making for the door of the library. Either Professor Snodgrass had failed to close it on entering, or somebody else had opened it subsequently. For it was certainly ajar by rather more than a chink now. Appleby was perhaps acting out of turn once more – for here again was something which, strictly regarded, was no business of his at all – but he nevertheless made no bones about going across the room at the double, and throwing the door as wide open as it would go. There was no doubt about the scent; it was faint and delicate, but undeniably present. Equally – if only for a moment – there was clear evidence of how it had, as it were, come on the air. The figure of a woman had disappeared round the curve of the quadrant corridor. Appleby hesitated, and decided not to follow. He really could not go pounding after somebody who might well enjoy a better right to be here than he did. Then he found that Professor Snodgrass was standing beside him, sniffing vigorously.

'Not a doubt of it,' Snodgrass said with satisfaction. 'Unmistakably camel.'

Chapter Five

'Then it was a white camel,' Appleby said, 'and it walked on two feet.'

'Puzzling thing.' Professor Snodgrass received this exasperated remark quite seriously. 'Might be a trick of the light, perhaps? In mirage conditions, I've seen them with up to eight. Feet, that is.'

'There was a woman at this door, and presumably she was listening to us.' Appleby pursued his plan of dogged rationality. 'A woman in white. Have you . . .'

'A woman in white? Fellow wrote a yarn called that. Not at all bad. Much better than modern stuff of the same sort.'

'No doubt.' Appleby felt no disposition to digress upon the literary merits of Wilkie Collins. 'Have you any idea why a woman dressed entirely in white should be wandering round Ledward?'

'None whatever. It sounds a shade eccentric to me.' Having produced this brilliant riposte, the Professor at once capped it. 'Do you think she might be impersonating a ghost?' He picked up the decanter, and held it interrogatively over his guest's glass.

'No more, thank you – although it's a capital port. May I ask whether you have many women in your household?'

'Lord no, my dear fellow. Lost interest in them years ago. And in a quiet country situation it just doesn't do.' Professor Snodgrass shook his head a shade nostalgically. 'Adrian found that.'

'Did he, indeed? I was thinking of servants, as a matter of fact.'

'Oh, I see. Not quite the same thing, eh? Not that one can't have what you might call an overlap.' Whether genuinely or not, the Professor's glance momentarily suggested a ripe Edwardian depravity. 'There's my cook, Mrs Gathercoal. Invaluable woman. Understands a *soufflé*. Set her to one for you, if you're kind enough to stay on. Manage you a bit of rough shooting, too. Brought your gun?'

The wandering course of these remarks, and much else in his host's conversation, might be the result, Appleby supposed, of their being offered in a large absence of mind. There could be no doubt that, as he talked, the old gentleman never ceased to *listen*. And it wasn't for those problematical personages whom Appleby was coming to judge rather thick on the ground. Women in white, for example, didn't interest the present guardian of Ledward Park in the least. His mind was entirely concentrated upon that imposing property's missing heir.

'And a couple of other women,' Snodgrass said. 'Housemaids, I suppose they'd be called. And, of course, there's my butler, Leonidas. Uncommon name, eh? Very decent one, too. I engaged him on the strength of it. Can't say he's turned out all that Spartan. Still, it puts one in mind of what was a damned good show. If the Phocians had just held on to that mountain path by Anopaea, it might even . . .'

'I suppose so.' Appleby judged the tactics of the battle of Thermopylae to be even more irrelevant than the literary accomplishment of the author of *The Woman in White*. 'Does Leonidas keep an eye on the Park as well as your own house?'

'Dear me, yes. They all have to lend a hand. And some of my outdoor people as well. Must stay shipshape.' Professor Snodgrass paused. 'But I was telling you about my nephew Adrian. Boring you, I expect.'

'Not at all. And, for that matter, you haven't told me very much. We were interrupted. South America, for instance. Your nephew spends a good deal of his time there?'

'He certainly used to.' It was conceivable that the Professor – unmindful of the uses of *Who's Who* – had glanced at Appleby with fleeting suspicion and surprise. 'We have family connections in more South American countries than one. In fact, both the Snodgrasses and the Beddoeses have. I daresay you may have heard of my maternal grandfather, Beddoes Beddoes. Known as the Liberator, in that part of the world. Liberated a pretty packet for himself, in a quiet way.' The Professor produced his hoarse chuckle. 'Still, a great patriot in his adoptive land, and so forth. Decapitated a pretty ugly dictator called Gozman Spinto with his own hand, they say, and then gave the place a constitution. Literally handed it over, handsomely bound in full morocco, to some ruffians he'd appointed vice-presidents and judges and senators and what have you. But really held all the strings himself up to the day of his death. Smart politician, was my grandfather Beddoes the Liberator.'

'And Adrian has also interested himself in politics there?'

'Decidedly – and fished in some deuced muddy waters, if you ask me. The boy has all the Beddoes spirit of adventure. He also has the Snodgrass brains. He needed both for that affair in Azuera. As revolutions go, a classic of its kind.'

'I think I remember what you're talking about. Adrian was in on that?'

'Master-minded it, my dear fellow. And then led the assault on the Ministry of War himself.'

'There was a certain ruthlessness to it, if I'm not mistaken.'

'Dear me, yes. I don't think Adrian actually took an axe to

anybody's neck. But he didn't precisely stay the hand of his supporters.'

'Did they remain his supporters for long?'

'Ten days or a fortnight, I think it was – and then young Adrian – he *was* young Adrian then – was on his travels again.'

'What has he been doing during the last ten years?'

'The last ten years?' For the first time, the conversable Professor Beddoes Snodgrass had hesitated. 'We haven't heard much of him, as a matter of fact. I don't know that we've heard anything at all.'

'So you simply keep this place going, and expect him to turn up? It seems rather strange to me – if I may say so – that with such a splendid patrimony in his own right your nephew should remain a wanderer on the face of the earth. For I take it that Ledward *is* Adrian's absolutely?'

'Of course it is. Not a doubt of it.'

'Doesn't his absence – or at least his complete silence added to that – produce any legal difficulties?'

'Nothing of the kind. There are trusts, and powers of thingummy, and so forth – all fixed up by the sharks. I have no difficulty at all.'

'Who would inherit Ledward if Adrian never came back – if he got himself killed in another palace revolution or military coup?'

How Professor Snodgrass might have responded to this outrageous curiosity was never to be known. For he had suddenly raised an arresting hand.

'Listen!' he said. 'Here he is.'

For seconds Appleby heard nothing at all. As his ear remained tolerably acute, he was inclined to suppose that the Professor was imagining things. Anybody, after all, who mounted so odd an annual occasion as Appleby had stumbled upon must be regarded as harbouring a certain liability in that direction. But in his supposition Professor Snodgrass's fortuitous guest proved wrong. It was simply that Professor Snodgrass's own ear – at least for the matter in hand – was very acute indeed. For now there *was* a sound. It was that of a car which was still a long way off. Perhaps it was simply passing in the night, and would come no nearer than the road upon which Appleby's own car was stranded. But in a moment this conjecture too was falsified. The car was coming up the drive.

'He's not quite on time,' Professor Snodgrass said. He had adopted a casual air which carried no conviction at all. It was plain that, whether fondly or not, he believed that his great moment had come. He had kept his promise by Adrian: the candle in the window, and much other welcoming ritual besides. And now, after many years, Adrian was keeping his promise by him.

Appleby's only impulse was to get out. If the car didn't herald the owner of Ledward at all – if it contained, for instance, a conscientious local policeman doing his best to keep an eye on what must by now be a notorious folly – then Professor Snodgrass's disillusion would be an uncomfortable thing to witness. If, on the other hand, Adrian Snodgrass had really and truly turned up, the resulting family occasion would equally not be an affair for a stranger to assist at. Adrian after ten years or more would not be quite the Adrian his uncle remembered, and the encounter might not, for one reason or another, run on the kind of lines the old gentleman had been envisaging. Appleby somehow couldn't believe in an agreeable Adrian Snodgrass. In a sense, no doubt, the Professor had enjoyed his long wardenship of Ledward Park, but he would surely have enjoyed it more if he had continued to receive, from time to time, some token of thanks or interest from its wandering heir. Moreover, unless he had been treating himself to the perverse enjoyment of putting on a dotard's turn, it semed likely that the Adrian who now chiefly existed in his memory was a very early Adrian indeed: perhaps even the small boy who had been photographed in soldier's uniform long ago.

Having decided so much, Appleby got to his feet. Discounting as much as possible the mere oddity of proposing to walk out into the night, he would take a firm conventional farewell of Professor Beddoes Snodgrass (not forgetting a further word of praise for the port) and depart resolutely from the house. And he decided to leave by the french window he had lately investigated. It would be more awkward still to run into the returning Adrian (if, again, conceivably it *was* he) before his own open front door.

'Not yet, my dear Appleby.' The Professor had made a gesture which invited his guest to resume his seat. 'I know you must be as eager to greet Adrian as I am. But it won't be proper quite yet.'

'Not proper?' Appleby was so astonished that he did actually sit down again. 'If it's really your nephew who is arriving, surely you are going straight out to welcome him?'

'Certainly not. You forget that this is his own house. He enters and takes possession of it. He enjoys, if he cares to, the refreshment laid out for him. It will then be for us to present ourselves. In a sense we shall be welcoming him. But it will be, on my part, as a kinsman who is a neighbour, and, on your part, as that kinsman's guest. Listen! The car must be a hired car. It's driving away again.'

This was true, and it was a circumstance that seemed to Appleby to negative the notion of an expostulating policeman. Whoever had simply been dropped at the front door of Ledward at such an hour plainly proposed to spend the rest of the night there. For the first time, Appleby found himself positively inclining to the view that Beddoes Snodgrass's dream was about to realize itself. But this only strengthened his own resolution to depart. So he once more rose, and this time advanced upon Professor Snodgrass with an outstretched hand.

'It has been a great pleasure to call upon you,' he said in what he hoped was a virtually hypnotic tone. 'But I must not intrude upon your family occasion. In fact, I will leave by the terrace. What a splendid port that is! Good night.'

'My dear fellow, must you go?' The Professor, to Appleby's relief, appeared to be politely masking surprise, and had even extended his own hand. 'Do drop in on me at my own place at any time. No point in standing on ceremony with a new neighbour, eh?'

'I shall be delighted,' Appleby said mendaciously, and made for the french window. It was perhaps because he was so decidedly not standing upon the order of his going – because, to put it crudely, he was in flight – that a second later he failed to pull up in time. He had opened the window, stepped briskly into the night, and collided violently with a more or less solid object. But it was not, in fact, an object so solid as to be immovable. It was now, indeed, supine on the terrace. And it was undoubtedly a man.

Appleby took no time at all to decide that here was one prowler too many. He pounced on the intruder not with any intention of assisting him to rise but in a determination to pin him to the ground. This resolution was only enhanced when he remarked, in the abundant light from within, that the lurking individual had chosen to attire himself in the garb of a clergyman. It was a form of disguise on the part of the criminal classes which he had always strongly reprobated.

'You'd better not struggle,' he said. 'I have a pretty good hold on you.'

'My dear Beddoes, you are being somewhat impetuous, are you not?'

Appleby let go hastily. The clergyman – who now quite plainly *was* a clergyman – sat up. And, at the same moment, Professor Snodgrass emerged on the terrace.

'That isn't Beddoes,' the Professor said prosaically. 'It's Sir John Appleby, my dear William. He's our new neighbour. At least I take it he's that. I suspect he has a notion there may be thieves around. I suppose him to imagine that he has apprehended one in your person. Appleby, this is our vicar, Dr Absolon. Shall we all go inside? William, you need a clothes-brush. Leonidas must find you one. He's coming over to the Park presently. Your visit is at a surprising hour – but timely, as a matter of fact. I'll tell you why, as soon as you've had a drink.'

'I don't know what you mean by a surprising hour.' Dr Absolon had risen and was dusting himself down. He was also regarding Appleby (whom he might reasonably have considered to be little better than a mad dog) with perfect charity. 'It's the hour you asked me to turn up at, after all.'

'Dear me!' The Professor appeared slightly disconcerted. 'Are you sure, my dear fellow?'

'Of course I'm sure. You said there was a strong probability of your nephew arriving, and that I ought to be here to welcome him on behalf of the parish.'

'Did I? In any case, it's very jolly of you, William, to have come across. And Adrian is certainly back at Ledward, I'm delighted to say. So come inside, both of you.'

Although conscious of thereby indicting himself of some infirmity of purpose, Appleby submitted, along with the new arrival, to this injunction. The odd pasture of affairs at Ledward was really too seducing to abandon. Had Professor Snodgrass, or had Professor Snodgrass not, really invited Dr Absolon to turn up at this unearthly hour? If he had, the manner in which he had now received the vicar suggested that he had forgotten all about it. Had Absolon (like other problematical persons earlier that night) been for some reason lurking outside the library when Appleby tumbled out on him? Or did that particular terrace constitute his normal route from his vicarage to the Park? As he framed these silent questions, Appleby found himself in possession of another glass of port. He regarded it without enthusiasm. He was again feeling hungry, and what he would chiefly have liked would have been to return to the dining-room, and there – whether in the company of Adrian Snodgrass or not – recruit himself from the collation provided. But it was clear that Adrian's uncle attached an almost sacramental significance to the returned wanderer's supping in august solitude. And probably he would regard the inside of an hour as the minimum time requisite for this refection. Appleby would have to put up with satisfying a purely intellectual appetite.

Resigned to this, he took a good look at Dr Absolon. He was a middle-aged man, and plainly in the enjoyment of a robust constitution and benign temperament. This latter endowment, indeed, he had decidedly required to carry him unperturbed through his recent upsetting experience. He seemed to bear Appleby no ill-will, but he was certainly eyeing him with some curiosity. Considering that this stranger had been abruptly presented to him as a new neighbour with a more or less obsessive interest in thieves, this was natural enough. Appleby decided further to expand his claim to the role.

'On this occasion last year,' he said firmly, 'the Professor had some reason to suppose that there might be thieves around. And this year – although I haven't so far alarmed him with the mention of it – I have had some reason to feel the same thing myself. I wonder, sir, whether you have seen or heard anything as you walked over to the Park?'

'Too dark to see even the nose on one's face. I simply aimed at the Professor's illuminations, and walked straight ahead. Lead, kindly Light, to Ledward, so to speak.' Absolon appeared to find this turn of phrase amusing rather than profane, for he laughed cheerfully. 'But I did hear something, as a matter of fact. Voices somewhere in the dark, and close to where my path joins the drive.'

'Do people normally move through that part of the park?'

'Oh, certainly. There are several paths that people in the local hamlets are let use quite freely. It was uncommonly late for anything of the kind. But I imagined there had been some junketing somewhere in the neighbourhood.'

'Ah – then they were rustic voices?'

'No, I don't think they were. No, decidedly they were not.'

'Cultivated voices, in fact?'

'I wouldn't say they were that, either.' Justifiably, the vicar seemed a little surprised at this inquisition. 'Come to think of it, I'd say they might be described as lower-class urban voices.'

'And just engaged in careless nocturnal chat?'

'That wasn't my impression, at all. What I seem to recall is two or three men, talking in low tones or whispering, as if to avoid all possibility of being overheard, but swearing at each other, and therefore raising their voices a little from time to time. I think one of them may have had a bicycle, since there was a sudden metallic sound which might have been a pedal scraping a wall in the dark. But certainly there were at least two men on foot, because I heard them go off more or less at a run.'

'You must be credited with a most discriminating ear, sir.' Appleby looked thoughtfully at Dr Absolon. 'Would you draw any conclusion from this encounter?'

'Thieves again, eh?' The Professor interrupted with this. 'But retreating, baffled, because the house is so brightly lit. I believe, my dear Appleby, I put that point to you earlier.'

'You did. But they mayn't have been baffled this time. Certainly we've taken no hand at baffling them. They may have made off with the Lord knows what, and they may have sounded cross to Dr Absolon because they were starting to quarrel over the booty.'

'This is very disturbing,' Dr Absolon said. He sniffed comfortably at his port. 'Anything of the sort would sadly mar the homecoming of your nephew, my dear Beddoes. Ought we, perhaps, to investigate?' As he made this suggestion, Absolon settled himself more deeply into his chair. 'A most vexatious thing!' he added. 'I appear not to have brought my pipe.'

'Then you must have a cigar.' Professor Snodgrass had risen hospitably to his feet. 'As for investigating, there is much to be said for it. Appleby, would you agree?'

'Most definitely. But it's not quite my place to take the initiative.'

'Quite so. Nor mine, either.' Having found and offered a cigar-box, the Professor was settling down again as for leisured chat. 'We must put the matter to Adrian, wouldn't you say? Report to him the slight uneasiness we feel. But not, of course, until the dear fellow has supped comfortably.'

'I hope he appears to be in good health?' Absolon asked.

'So do I. I haven't yet seen him, you know. As I've explained to Appleby, I feel Adrian should begin by taking undisturbed possession of the house.'

'I see.' Absolon looked puzzled; it was apparent that he found this whimsy as odd as Appleby did. 'In fact, it is not yet quite certain that your nephew *has* arrived? It may be somebody quite different?'

'Stuff and nonsense, my dear William! This is Adrian's birthday, and there is a compact between us. Of course it is he. He simply drove up, and dismissed his conveyance. Appleby and I heard it quite clearly. Adrian will by now be in the dining-room.'

'But has he not always been something of a jester, Beddoes? What if he has sent some wholly unsuitable person to keep this tryst with you?' Dr Absolon, who was beginning to strike Appleby as possessing as curious a turn of mind as the Professor himself, paused consideringly. 'A mistress, for example?

It has never been clear to me that your nephew's morals were particularly good. What if it is some outrageous Paphian girl, my dear fellow, who is scoffing whatever is upon your outspread board?'

'This is no occasion for foolery, William.'

'Perfectly true.' The vicar paused to draw appreciatively upon his cigar. 'For let me mention another hazard. It is many years since you saw Adrian; and your faculties, you know, are not quite what they were. My own acquaintance with him was slight, and my memory of him is a very general one. And he can never have been known to your butler, Simonides.'

'Leonidas.'

'To be sure. But my point is that, in this queer business we are involved in, there exist almost ideal conditions for successful impersonation. This ritual return, with its extravagant build-up of expectation on your part, must have the effect of rendering you wholly uncritical. Credulous, in fact, and ready to swallow anything. Sir John, don't you agree with me?'

'There is some cogency in your line of thought. But I don't think the Professor is very happy with it.'

This was an understatement. Absolon had certainly not paused to put much tact into the role of candid friend; and Professor Snodgrass was not taking kindly the suggestion that his wits were so decayed as to render him incapable of identifying his own nephew. That the vicar's remarks were offered with perfect good humour and a kind of genial pastoral concern probably rendered them all the more annoying. Certainly the Professor retorted upon them with some heat.

'William, the truth about you is that you spend too little time writing your sermons, and too much reading mystery stories. If you only came over to talk rubbish to me . . .'

'But I didn't. I came to make sure that no successful imposture takes place. For some years, I don't think people had a clear notion of what you were about on this annual occasion. But now, as I happen to know, the whole neighbourhood has more or less got the hang of it – and it may well have spread a good deal farther than that. The very least that you must expect sooner or later is either some tiresome joke, or the much worse annoyance of a kind of Tichborne Claimant. I believe that imposture of that kind, my dear chap, has to be killed at once and on the ground. Let it take the air, and the devil's own mischief may follow. Sir John, you would again agree with me?'

'Certainly.' Appleby was allowing himself to look with some astonishment at the vicar. 'And you feel, sir, that you are the man to make that early kill?'

'I could have a pretty good shot at it. And if anything of the sort is a possibility, I judged that Beddoes would be the better of a friend standing by. I was supposing, you know, that there would be nobody else here – except, perhaps, that fellow Leonidas. So I decided that Beddoes's invitation should be accepted.'

'You would nevertheless agree that, if somebody is indeed at supper in the dining-room at this moment, he is much more likely to be the genuine Adrian Snodgrass than a pretender?'

'Oh, dear me, yes! I merely claim that there must be some substantial possibility of vexatious foolery, or of deception. Beddoes, I hope you are not upset by these cautions and suspicions of mine?'

The Professor, it seemed to Appleby, was less upset than bewildered. He had stood up to Absolon stoutly enough, but – if only obscurely – his confidence could be felt as flickering. Or was it rather that the vicar's unexpected onslaught had caused him to lose command of a role, so that he was searching round to recover it? Flushed, whether with indignation or alarm, he made only an unsuccessful attempt at utterance. Before he could try again, the library door had opened as library doors can only open under the hand of a trained manservant. The figure revealed was heavily bearded, and he was not dressed as butlers are dressed in the advertisements. Nevertheless Appleby was instantly assured that this stiff and ponderous figure was Leonidas, who had been received into the service of an eminent retired military historian on account of his name's recalling the hero of Thermopylae.

If Leonidas was surprised to find that his employer had

45

company, nothing of it showed on features which were at once professionally impassive and so unprofessionally hirsute. If his glance did pause on Appleby, it was for no longer than was wholly decorous. And then he addressed Professor Snodgrass with an impassive formality.

'Mr Snodgrass is in residence, sir,' Leonidas said.

Chapter Six

The first reaction to Leonidas's announcement came, oddly enough, from the Reverend Doctor Absolon, so comfortably relaxed over his port and his cigar. It took the form, indeed, of no more than a flicker of the eyebrows, directed at Appleby. For a moment Appleby supposed that what was being suggested was merely a sense of mild amusement at a form of words which might have been deemed more appropriate to the movements of a duke or marquess than of one so addicted as Adrian Snodgrass appeared to be to the role of a very private gentleman. But then Appleby divined that it was something quite different that Absolon wanted to convey. Leonidas, he was indicating, had taken the identity of the new arrival for granted. Adrian Snodgrass was totally unknown to him, so here might be, as it were, the Tichborne Claimant in person. And the Claimant had won his first small round. A preliminary assumption was established. Professor Snodgrass had only to behave in as dotty a fashion as he appeared abundantly capable of, and the fellow might get away with goodness knew what.

But Absolon was very tolerably dotty himself. Beneficed clergymen of the Church of England ought not to drift around scattering bizarre suspicions among their parishioners. And the suspicion was, of course, fantastic. Something quite sufficiently surprising had happened. Adrian Snodgrass was indeed in residence.

'Quite so,' the Professor was saying. 'Precisely so, Leonidas. My guest and I heard Mr Snodgrass arrive. You have presented yourself?'

46

'Yes, sir. I came over to the Park at the time you directed, and very shortly afterwards Mr Snodgrass rang the dining-room bell. I found him at table, sir. I uncorked the champagne.'

'Excellent! And he appears to be in good spirits?'

'Decidedly, sir. Most affable, he was. A jocose gentleman, if the word may be permitted me. I followed your instructions, explained that I was in your service at the Old Dower House, and that you had said I was to venture to wait upon him. He asked at once if I would consider being employed by himself at what he termed a stiffer screw. I took this as evidence of a facetious disposition. He then told me to put a second bottle of champagne on the ice.'

'The devil he did!' It was Dr Absolon who uttered this un-clerical ejaculation. 'Well, well!'

'The which I did at once.' Leonidas looked with a kind of respectful disapproval at the vicar. 'I presume Mr Snodgrass had it in mind that he would presently be joined by the Professor. In fact, he indicated as much.'

'Good!' Professor Snodgrass said. 'Capital! Just what did he say, Leonidas?'

'Verbatim, sir?'

'Certainly verbatim. I am most anxious to hear the dear lad's words.'

'He said, sir, to send the old fellow along at any time. I understand myself to be following the injunction – if that be an agreeable term, sir – now.'

Not unnaturally, this piece of information produced a small pause. Appleby wondered whether Professor Snodgrass was experiencing a certain difficulty in swallowing it. He also con-jectured that Leonidas had taken the suggestion of changed employment and a higher wage seriously. This would account for a certain cautiously menial insolence which the bearded butler was permitting himself.

'Adrian appears affectionately disposed,' Absolon offered drily. 'He does not propose to stand upon ceremony.'

'But first,' Leonidas continued with satisfaction, 'he invited me to take a glass of madeira. I was honoured, and complied.'

'Quite right,' Professor Snodgrass said. 'The gesture was a

very proper one on my nephew's part. Did he say anything else, Leonidas?'

'Well, yes.' Very rapidly, Leonidas gave his employer what Appleby found himself judging a wary glance. 'He asked me whether I knew who the girl was.'

'The girl, Leonidas!'

'He said he had glimpsed a female person, sir. As he entered the house.'

'Did he happen to say anything,' Appleby interposed, 'about the female person's being in white?'

'No.' Leonidas looked at Appleby with open disapprobation. 'Mr Snodgrass did not animadvert upon the person's attire.'

'Have you yourself glimpsed this woman?'

'No.'

'Or anybody else, since you came over to the Park?'

For a moment Leonidas made no reply. Instead, he looked at his employer as if reproaching him for having suddenly descended to keeping low company. Then he brought himself again to glance at Appleby.

'No,' Leonidas said.

There was another pause.

'Dr Absolon,' the Professor said pacifically to his butler, 'has been aware of what might be called suspicious movements out in the park. And so, it appears, nearer the house, has Sir John Appleby. Sir John, by the way, Leonidas, is a new neighbour. It is a little worrying, you know. We did have that alarm at this time last year. But, of course, the lights keep actual burglars, and so forth, away.'

'I am afraid that has never been my opinion, sir. Contrariwise, indeed.' Leonidas's disaffection appeared to be growing. 'A residence like this, all lit up and deserted, has never made sense to me, I'm bound to say. I wouldn't do it myself, not for a single night, I wouldn't, not for a waggon-load of nephews, or monkeys either. It's asking for suspicious happenings, it is. And when suspicious happenings happen, it's the servants that get the worst of it. In good service, such oughtn't to happen at all. To my mind, if I may be permitted to obtrude such a thing.'

This highly improper speech naturally produced adverse reactions in the three gentlemen to whom, indifferently, it had been proffered. Dr Absolon's glance contrived to express the conviction that, if one did employ a pampered butler, it was exactly this sort of impertinence that one must expect sooner or later. Appleby found himself wondering whether here was not so much a pampered butler as a clever rogue. And Professor Snodgrass himself appeared to feel that some mild rebuke was requisite.

'Thank you, Leonidas, you may go,' Professor Snodgrass said – for all the world like an employer in a Victorian novel. 'In fact, you may retire to bed.'

It is probable that, upon this command, Leonidas gave a cold bow. But only probable, since nobody was ever actually to know. For, much as if the Professor's words had been a cue-line in some old-fashioned melodrama, they had been instantly followed by a sudden deluge of darkness. The library remained, indeed, faintly lit by the dying fire. But throughout the room, as also in the corridor beyond the open door where Leonidas still stood, every light had been simultaneously extinguished. All Ledward Park was again as Appleby had first encountered it: a mere realm of Chaos and Old Night. Of Chaos in particular. For upon the inky gloom there immediately succeeded what might have been a nicely calculated crescendo of alarming, even of spinechilling, sounds. First there was an angry shout, then pounding feet, a crash of splintering glass, a woman's high-pitched scream, the shattering reverberation of a fire-arm discharged in a confined space. And then silence was entire again.

Part Two The Small Hours

Chapter Seven

It could at least be said of Leonidas that, in this emergency, he had his wits about him. He had stepped swiftly across the library, and within seconds lit he candles in a three-branched candlestick.

'On this side of the house, that was,' he said. 'The drawing-room, it might have come from. I suppose, sir' – he had turned to Professor Snodgrass – 'you wouldn't have that old revolver of yours handy in this room?'

'Of course not, Leonidas. But there are four of us, and we must tackle whatever mischief is afoot. William, you agree with me?'

'Most certainly – and I can see that Sir John does. The question would appear to be whether we scatter, or go forward in a body. I am inclined to think that we may *be* bodies if we advance together along that very awkward quadrant corridor. For I suppose that robbery with violence is what confronts us.'

'That seems probable enough.' Appleby had taken the candelabrum from Leonidas, and was walking towards the door. 'But, if so, the robbery is likely to be over, and the robbers to be departing rather rapidly now. I propose returning to the hall. Leonidas, if I call to you from there, you are to come out and make your way to the switch-board, wherever that may be. It is probable that somebody has merely thrown out the main switch. Get it in again. Or, if fuses have been tampered with, do what you can. Professor Snodgrass, I would ask you and the vicar to remain here for the moment.' Appleby was making no bones about taking charge in the emergency. It was his sort of thing, after all. 'But I think I noticed a telephone in this room. If so, be so kind as to call the police at once. Tell them there has been shooting. It will get them out of bed. Right? Now I'll take a look around.'

He walked rapidly down the corridor. It wasn't a place in which to loiter. But almost immediately he heard footsteps behind him – footsteps and a muted tap-tap which he knew to be produced by Professor Snodgrass's rubber-tipped stick.

'I would really rather you remained in the library,' he said, without looking round. 'Situations like this are quite familiar to me, you know.'

'I think it probable that I have been under fire quite as often as you have.' There was a surprising snap in Snodgrass's voice, so that momentarily he sounded a much younger man. 'And I have to know what has happened to Adrian.'

'Very well.' Appleby was looking fixedly ahead of him. It was still into nothing but absolute darkness. He remembered that the corridor gave not directly on the imposing colonnaded hall, but on a room of moderate size which came in between. And here it was, floating glimmeringly into view through an open door. He hadn't paused on first passing through it, and he didn't pause now. Only he saw from its glimpsed furnishings that it would probably be known as the music room. *Facing the music*, he told himself, and in half-a-dozen further strides was in the hall. The Professor was now shoulder to shoulder with him – which was remarkably good going on a stick.

The two men stood between two of the columns that soared to the scarcely visible ornate ceiling. Merely between these, there would have been room without crowding for four or five men more. Who had once talked, Appleby asked himself, of feeling like a mouse in a cathedral? Here – holding aloft these three wax candles – one felt more like a glow-worm in a forest: an enchanted forest, in which the tree-trunks were a frozen honey and the foliage hammered gold. A cold breath blew through the forest. Appleby wondered why.

'The drawing-room,' he said in a low voice. 'We'll try that first.'

The dead man lay prone on the floor, with his head in the drawing-room and his heels in the hall. Even by candlelight his deadness didn't seem arguable, since a bullet had emerged

– not tidily – through the back of his head. His left arm was crumpled beneath him; his right was outstretched as if to reach into the room, and in its hand was grasped a heavy brass poker. It was from the cavernous darkness beyond the body that the small chill breeze was blowing.

Appleby had set the candelabrum down on the marble floor – inconsequently aware, as he did so, of its decorous Georgian elegance. This damned house, he reflected, is full of loot. His hands busied themselves expertly with the body. He straightened up.

'If he were on the operating-table at this moment,' he said to Snodgrass, 'there wouldn't be a hope for him. But we must still keep our priorities right. I'll give Leonidas that shout.'

The shout rapidly produced footfalls, the glimmer of a match guarded behind a cupped hand, and then the bearded face of the butler in the chiaroscuro thus created. It wasn't, Appleby told himself, the face of a frightened man; one didn't warm to Leonidas, but there seemed to be plenty of stuffing in him. And of his employer there could be no question. Snodgrass was agitated, and no doubt in acute anxiety as to the identity of the shot man. But the possibility of further shooting didn't alarm him.

'Leonidas, go back to that telephone, and summon your local doctor at once.'

'The telephone appears to be out of order, sir. Dr Absolon has just discovered so on trying to call the police. If there has been a robbery, one must suppose the line to have been cut.'

'There's been more than a robbery, as you can see,' Appleby said grimly. 'Is there a car here at the Park?'

'My own car is in the stable-yard. I save time by coming across in it.'

'Good. Then go and fetch the doctor yourself. As fast as you can possibly manage. And have a call put through to the police from his house.'

'Very good, sir. And the lights?'

'Yes – give a moment to that as you go. But don't let it hold you up, if you can't get them on instantly. And take one of these candles.'

Leonidas hurried off. It was only when his footsteps had died away that Appleby knelt down again, and for a moment half-turned the body over.

'Snodgrass,' he asked gently, 'is this your nephew?'

'Yes.' The Professor spoke in a low voice, which for a moment broke into a sob. 'And in the very moment...' He checked himself. 'It is Adrian,' he said tonelessly. 'Is it quite certain that nothing can be done?'

'Quite certain, I am afraid.' Appleby lowered the body again to its first position. 'Take a candle,' he said, 'and go into that bedroom near the dining-room. Bring a sheet. It will be all that is required.'

It was just as Snodgrass was stooping to do as he was bid that the lights snapped on. The two men stared at each other, momentarily dazzled, and then both looked down at the corpse. It was, somehow, the most macabre moment yet. Appleby was glad that Adrian Snodgrass's face was concealed again. The shot had been fired straight into it – so that the crime seemed to cry out the additional horror of a revolting brutality. Beddoes Snodgrass turned away, and now it was slowly and painfully again that he made his way across the great marble expanse of the hall. It was as if his years, and more than his years, had returned to him.

'Somebody has been killed?' It was Dr Absolon who asked the question. He had emerged through the music room, and had now stopped dead at the spectacle before him. 'Snodgrass's nephew?'

'I'm afraid so.' Appleby suddenly remembered the somewhat odd speculations in which this country clergyman had been indulging. 'But I could almost believe he had made the identification too confidently. There's no need for you to look – indeed, I'd rather the body wasn't disturbed again until the doctor and the police have seen it – but the features have suffered pretty badly.'

'I see.' Absolon (who might be momentarily shocked by the fact of death, but presumably was professionally immune from being puzzled by it) knelt down by the body, put a hand gently on its shoulder, and then stood up again and unobtrusively crossed himself. 'Would you say,' he asked curiously, 'that he has been killed just as he *has* been killed precisely with that end in view?'

'Preventing his uncle from positively identifying him?'

'Preventing *anybody* from doing so with certainty.'

'It's conceivable, I suppose.'

'Or at least may that be the actual consequence? May it never be certainly known who this unfortunate man is?'

'I'd have thought that barely possible.' Appleby was again fleetingly conscious of something idiosyncratic in the mental operations of the vicar of Ledward. Perhaps they really were coloured by an obsessive reading of mystery stories. The archetypal reader of such things, after all, was popularly thought of as a blameless parson with long afternoons to put in on a vicarage lawn. 'It would be something extremely unusual – in England, at least. Particularly where there's the presumption of a specific identity. We have every reason to suppose that here is Adrian Snodgrass – an elusive character, perhaps, but of some position in the world, and to be read about, if you care to, in *Who's Who*. Of course, *Who's Who* doesn't record his dentist. But we can probably run him to earth.'

' "We"?'

'You catch me out there.' Appleby might have been laughing if propriety hadn't appeared to forbid. 'I've passed my active days among policemen, and ended up running a certain number of them. I still talk like a policeman.'

'And act like one too – and very convincingly. Do you know, I find that reassuring?' Dr Absolon gazed candidly at Appleby across the body of the dead man. 'Otherwise, I shouldn't find your presence here tonight altogether unalarming. Beddoes seems only to have the vaguest notion of who you are, or where you've turned up from, or why. You are the mysterious stranger who has been the first to find the body.' Absolon paused. 'But I see, my dear sir, that you judge me flippant. What has become of Beddoes?'

'Professor Snodgrass has gone to the other side of the house to find a sheet. He ought to be back by now – but I suspect he is under some strain, and has sat down for a few minutes to rest and recollect himself. I suggest that you and I take a look at this drawing-room.' And Appleby moved forward, skirting the body. 'We can keep an eye on one another,' he added drily.

'Very well.' But Dr Absolon was looking thoughtfully down at the poker in the dead man's hand. 'Do you know, I'd have expected that to go flying as he fell?'

'Indeed? That has been your experience, in cases in which persons carrying or brandishing weapons have been dropped by a revolver-shot as they ran?'

'My dear sir, now you are making fun of me.' The vicar was not at all offended. 'But let me make one more observation in the character of Dr Watson. I am convinced, my dear Holmes, that there have been thieves in this room.'

If a joke had been any more appropriate to the circumstances than a laugh, this wouldn't have been a bad one. A resourceful novelist might have declared that the drawing-room was like a place hit by a tornado. In one large sash-window there were only a few jagged and evil-looking spears and sickles of glass, as if somebody had been sufficiently in a hurry to chance making an exit that way under the impulsion of a hurtling shoulder. Of the smaller *objets d'art* with which the place had been stacked and littered Appleby judged at a rapid glance that about a third had disappeared. And something more striking had disappeared as well. Over the mantel-shelf only an expanse of faintly discoloured white enamel showed where lately there had hung a landscape by Claude Gelée, called le Lorrain. It had been, Appleby recalled, a View of the Campagna, with some banditti – no doubt supplied by one of the Courtois brothers – lurking rather unconvincingly in a corner. Now one could imagine these ruffians as having broken out of their own picture, grabbed at it frame and all, and made off with whatever they could hastily tip into a couple of sacks.

'It isn't surprising that there's a bit of a draught,' Absolon said. He walked over to the shattered window. 'But this isn't like the private wing, you know. No terrace. We're simply perched above the basement storey. Booty and all, they had to find some means of taking a twelve-foot drop. It can't have been a planned exit this way. They were surprised – and bolted in an unpremeditated and highly hazardous fashion. What's the odds they got at least a gash or two from all that flying glass? There will be blood down there, if you ask me.' Having peered briefly out into the night, the vicar turned round to look at Appleby. 'But why did the lights go out?'

'My dear Dr Absolon, that is a question to which I don't doubt that you can supply me with more answers than one.'

'One needs an answer that fits into the simplicity of the thing.'

'Its simplicity? Are you sure you don't mean its nonsensicalness?'

'Essentially its simplicity, surely. On this night of the year alone, the Snodgrasses keep, as it were, open house. Anybody can walk in – and be sure of finding nobody around. By "anybody" we have to mean, of course, anybody who knows just how our friend the Professor's annual ritual has evolved. Well, in they come, having a mind to the Claude I see you mourning, and to much else. Unfortunately, what nobody except Beddoes himself believes will ever really happen *has* happened. Adrian Snodgrass has turned up; he has sat down to the waiting meal; his uncle's faithful old servitor (I refer to that patent rascal, Leonidas, my dear Appleby) presents himself, opens a bottle of champagne, and makes his way – full of glad tidings – to the library. The thieves, meanwhile, have arrived. Adrian hears something suspicious; something so suspicious that he picks up a poker and goes to investigate. He appears at the door of this room. The criminals panic; one of them shoots at him point-blank, and they make a disorderly retreat through the window. Appleby, don't you see it that way?'

'I fear I lack your amateur *élan*, sir. I shouldn't dream of asserting that I see it at all.' Appleby offered this reply absently, since he was prowling restlessly and enquiringly around the room. 'However, it may well be that you have arrived at some part of the truth. You were asking yourself, by the way, why the lights went out.'

'They went out as they did – with a shattering simultaneity – simply because they *could* so go out. It has been Beddoes's whim so to order matters that he can turn *on* every light in the house at the flick of a single switch. So they can similarly be turned off, and therefore . . .'

'My dear Vicar, there is nothing singular about that. Almost every lighting system is arranged in that fashion.'

'Is that so? I am bound to admit I have never enquired. But my main point remains unaffected. There can be safety in sudden darkness where lawless behaviour is in question. The criminals had one of their number at the strategic point, wherever it may be. And he switched off the lights the moment he was aware that Adrian Snodgrass was alerted, and that danger was therefore imminent.'

'There is much to be said for your reading of the matter.' Appleby had come to a halt, and was now looking at Dr Absolon with attention. 'But I wonder whether it can be made to accommodate something else?'

'There *is* something else?'

'Well, for me there is. You see, it was I alone who saw her. The woman in white. But I think you too heard her scream.'

Chapter Eight

But now there was a new sound to be heard: one less definite than a scream, but somehow equally unnerving. Professor Snodgrass's uncertain footsteps, and the dull tap of Professor Snodgrass's stick on marble were elements in it. But so was a species of sobbing respiration, and what sounded like a muttering or babbling of broken sentences. And then Snodgrass was in the drawing-room. He had turned deathly pale – a state which might be accounted for by the fact that he had again had to skirt his cherished nephew's dead body. But he had also been reduced – momentarily, at least – to a condition of painful incoherence. He looked about him, stammering and feebly gesticulating. It was an awkward and painful confrontation.

'I'm afraid,' Appleby said, 'that a good deal has gone.' He had concluded that it was the ravaged state of this richly furnished and adorned apartment that had dealt the guardian of Ledward Park a culminating blow.

'Gone! He's gone?' Snodgrass had plainly misunderstood. 'But I must see him! Call him – call him at once. Find ...' He broke off with a bewilderment of his head, as if he had suddenly been unable to find a word, or a name.

'Leonidas?' Absolon said.

'Yes, yes. I must speak to him. What have you done with him?'

'I gave him an order,' Appleby said. 'This is a situation, I'm afraid, in which we can't stand upon ceremony. The telephone line has been cut. I've sent your man in his car for a doctor – and the police.'

'The doctor will be able to do nothing for your nephew,' Absolon said gently. 'But the police may catch . . .'

'Yes, William, yes. The murderers. The thieves. The thieves have killed him, haven't they? They've killed Adrian?' Suddenly Professor Snodgrass produced an extraordinary sound in his throat, so that Appleby expected him to fall senseless to the floor as the consequence of some cardiac or circulatory disaster. But Snodgrass only slumped into a chair. 'But I've seen them!' he cried. 'Can you understand? *I've seen them!*'

'They're still here?' Absolon asked sharply – and looked swiftly round as if in search of a likely weapon. Then he shook his head. 'Beddoes, calm yourself, for God's sake. The ruffians have bolted through that window. It's against reason that they should have come back. There's no danger. Appleby here will tell you so. And your nephew's death is our only real calamity.'

'Yes. Yes, of course.' The Professor made an effort to control himself, and wholly failed. 'In the bedroom,' he said hoarsely. 'Where I went for a sheet, as . . . as that man told me to.' He pointed wildly at Appleby. 'I was unnerved. I behaved like a poltroon, cowering by the door. And then I heard your voice, William, and ran to join you. *Ran.*' And Professor Snodgrass, having reiterated in this way what is a soldier's ugliest word, was suddenly quite still.

'It was only prudent,' Appleby said quietly. 'But I think you may have been mistaken. One's imagination can play tricks on one in circumstances like these. Remain where you are for a moment, while I go and see.'

'My dear sir . . .' Absolon began urgently. But he was addressing the back of another running man. For Appleby was out of the drawing-room and crossing Ledward's bleakly splendid hall at the double.

The odd lay-out of the mansion's principal apartments took him once more through the dining-room. Fleetingly, he glimpsed disorder. The single chair which had been set for the long-lost Adrian Snodgrass had been overturned, as if too hastily thrust backwards. It was a fine Hepplewhite chair, and its fretted lateral members had been fractured. The silver ice-bucket had rolled across the floor. A shattered champagne glass lay in a small puddle on the dark walnut table. *It all adds up*, Appleby told himself, and ran on without pause to the bedroom. The door was open. He went straight through. It was very much a moment recalling old times.

Anticlimax succeeded. Unless comically under the bed, or hidden in a wardrobe, there was nobody in the room. The intruders – if intruders there had been other than in the aged Professor's febrile fancy – had not lingered to explain themselves. And the good order of the place was quite undisturbed. The expensive pyjamas were still laid out on the bed. It was still possible to distinguish the hump of the hot-water bottle. The feet it had been designed to warm – Appleby thought grimly – were now fast chilling for good.

But *not* quite undisturbed. There was one single object which was in disarray. A picture had been wrenched from the wall, and now lay, face downwards, on the carpet. It had not gone the way of the Claude, one had to suppose, because somebody had been constrained to drop it and run. There had been a lot of running at Ledward just recently.

Appleby stooped, picked up the painting, and set it against the wall. He stared at it, perplexed. This wasn't a Claude. It wasn't a Poussin. It wasn't a Reynolds, a Gainsborough, or even a Romney. It was the sort of more than indifferent portrait of a lady (*circa* 1860, Appleby judged) that family piety hangs in places of semi-seclusion in great country houses.

John Appleby – those familiar wih his career will learn without surprise – had as a Boy Scout been particularly distinguished at what is called Kim's Game. Kim's Game consists in enumerating as many as possible of a miscellaneous assemblage of objects briefly glimpsed shortly before. Appleby found himself involved in this game now. Earlier that night, he had viewed the drawing-room at Ledward in its unviolated state. Minutes ago, he had viewed it again when a large variety of show-pieces of one sort and another had been raped from it. He was trying to call up a representative assemblage of those now missing, and an answering assemblage of those left behind – and to compare the artistic worth (and monetary value) of the two groups. This was a rather special and difficult variant of Kim's Game. But he found that he could arrive at very tolerable results. The thieves had known their stuff. It was extremely improbable that, so far as pictures went, they should have supposed that, next after Claude's Campagna with Banditti, they should go for this feebly delineated Victorian lady. So here was another component in what might be called the sheer-nonsense side of the affair into which the bad behaviour of a gear-lever had precipitated him.

And now he had better return to his companions. The local G.P. ought to be turning up any time now, and so ought the police. As far as the corpse went, the doctor's duties would be merely formal. But he might do something useful in the matter of the sadly disordered state of Professor Snodgrass. Give him a shot of something, or at least a couple of pills, that would get him some sleep and into reasonable shape for the morning. Not that the police wouldn't want to extract a statement from him here and now. And from Appleby himself, for that matter, and from the worthy Dr Absolon as well. And Leonidas. And of course there was the woman in white, if they could find her. Perhaps she was lurking in the house. Perhaps she inhabited some attic suite, unknown to anybody – and had so done for years. Appleby had no fancy for searching Ledward. It was a job that could absorb a long week-end. The police had better turn a posse on to it.

Perhaps it was the thought of the woman in white that reminded Appleby about getting hold of a sheet. He had better himself accomplish the mission upon which the Professor had been abortively despatched. He would simply take the upper sheet from this bed. To cover the dead body with that would have a decent appropriateness, after all.

Addressing himself to this, he became aware of a sheet where a sheet shouldn't be. There seemed to be a sheet – a crumpled sheet – *under* the bed . . .

And Appleby stood back.

'I think you might as well come out,' he said.

It is not very easy for a woman to emerge from beneath a gentleman's bed – even a deceased gentleman's bed – into the arms of a retired policeman and retain anything much of the quality known as presence. But the woman in white managed something like this. She was tall and dark; she was haggard and by no means still quite young; and she was not properly to be described as dressed in white at all. For what must be called her dress was a sophisticated and multitudinously coloured affair of barbaric suggestion, and over this she had simply swathed herself in a white plastic mackintosh. Or as such Appleby described it to himself, while reflecting that it might well be something more expensive than that. If a woman does emerge from under a bed – except in some stage farce of polite adultery – one somehow expects her to be of unassuming station: a pilfering housemaid, say, who has bolted for cover. This woman wasn't at all like that. She might have been described as entirely *en suite* with the restrained but unmistakable opulence of Ledward Park. Appleby found that this circumstance was some way from moderating the exasperation which was threatening to become his main response (improperly, no doubt) to an affair the pivot of which was, after all, a revolting murder.

'Madam,' he said, 'I wonder whether you would care to explain yourself?'

'Explain myself? Why should I? I live here.'

'I really don't think that can be quite true. You live, it seems to me, some little way off. Not really at a distance, but beyond the boundaries of this park.'

'You know nothing about me.'

'I know that you have just behaved in an uncommonly eccentric way – which is something, I must admit, that does rather blend you with the Ledward scene. But it's my point that, on a perfectly fine night, you can have donned that staring white garment only out of prudence when proposing to walk along a high road in the dark. In other words, you have appeared from somewhere in the neighbourhood, and have been lurking around this house for purposes best known to yourself. You produce the idiotic lie that you live here . . .'

'I ought to have said haunt here. In imagination I spend much time at Ledward. It is my home by right.'

'Why should you hide under a bed in your home by right?'

'I didn't like the appearance of those men.' The woman in white looked sombrely at Appleby. 'Did you?'

'I haven't had an opportunity to form an opinion, madam. And now, would you mind dropping all those riddles? Something very grave indeed has happened at Ledward, as I think you must know. The police will be arriving at any moment, and they will certainly require you to give an account of yourself. Therefore . . .'

'An account of myself? They know me perfectly well. I am a magistrate.'

'I assure you they will be particularly interested in a magistrate who scrambles under beds. But may I really appeal to you for a little sense? I've been a policeman myself. Rightly or wrongly, I feel I have a certain duty to do what I can to render this affair intelligible. So may I begin at the beginning, and ask you your name?'

'I am Mrs Anglebury – Cytherea Anglebury. I ought to be Mrs Snodgrass.' The woman in white produced this surprising statement quite flatly. Adrian Snodgrass's wife.'

'Mrs Anglebury, you do know, don't you, that Adrian Snodgrass is dead? In fact, you cried out almost at the moment he was killed?'

'Of course I know that Adrian is dead. Of course I know that he has been killed. It was I who killed him.' Mrs Anglebury frowned. 'Wasn't it? It's what I came to do. So I suppose I did it.'

'You are saying something very serious indeed. May I ask what you have done with the weapon?'

'The weapon? I have no idea. I quite forget.' Mrs Anglebury felt in the pockets of her mackintosh. 'Nothing here but a cigarette case. Do you smoke?'

That Appleby would have found any reply to this is uncertain. For suddenly a new voice – a man's – spoke from the doorway behind him.

'Hello, Mum,' it said cheerfully. 'I've come to take you home.'

It was a very young man who had entered the bedroom. He might be in his first term at Oxford, or his last term at a public school. His hair was moderately long rather than moderately short; he was dressed in patched jeans and a nondescript upper garment which he probably regarded as an impenetrable social disguise rendering him indistinguishable from a barrow-boy; yet you couldn't have mistaken him class-wise, or supposed him other than precisely what he was. Appleby felt, at the moment, all for a little straightness and wholesome simplicity. He felt uncomfortable about the part he must himself presently play. He cursed the splendour of Ledward's basilican hall, which could lead you from the front door to this part of the house unnoticing of certain grisly appearances masked by those great alabaster shafts. The lad didn't yet know that anything was amiss – or amiss, at least (so Appleby guessed), except in a sadly familiar fashion. This nice young man had a mother who was rather badly crazed. And, of course, badly crazed people can do sadly grisly things.

The young man was now looking at Appleby in an alerted way. He must be sufficiently familiar with the set-up at Ledward to know that here was somebody who normally had nothing to do with the place. He was about to call Appleby 'sir' – and to challenge him firmly enough. He was continuing to look very straight at Appleby. And it was a gaze that Appleby had a sudden strange sense of having met before.

'I'm afraid I've rather barged in, sir,' the young man said. 'My name's David Anglebury. I sometimes pick up my mother here. She enjoys a bit of a walk at night, and then I collect her in the car.'

'Yes, of course.' It was as he produced this meaningless phrase that Appleby realized he was speaking to a Snodgrass. Where he had seen these eyes before was in the photograph of a small boy in a soldier's suit. 'My name's Appleby,' Appleby said, and was conscious that he had rather tumbled out these words. 'I'm a stranger, and here by pure chance. Your mother and I have just met.'

'I was under the bed,' Mrs Anglebury said.

'How do you do?' It was with practised promptness that David Anglebury obliterated his mother's bizarre remark. 'Do you happen to know, sir, whether Mr Snodgrass has really turned up? I expect you've heard about his birthday, and so on. Every year we're interested to know if he has come home. It's what's brought my mother over, I expect. Mr Snodgrass – Adrian Snodgrass – and she are old friends.'

'Yes, of course.' Appleby didn't think it too bright to have reiterated this. He had just heard the sound of a car – perhaps two cars – approaching the house. 'Mr Snodgrass has arrived,' he said, 'and not more than an hour ago. But I ought to say *did* arrive.'

'He's gone away again?'

'In a sense, yes. He's dead.'

It had been an indecent stroke – but when surrounded by infuriating mystery and muddle one must play one's cards as one can. Appleby's eyes, steadily on the eyes of the young man, took in a moment of horror. That was natural enough. But had it been a moment of terror as well?

'He's *dead*? He was ill?'

'I'm sorry, Mr Anglebury. This isn't at all pleasant. There appears to have been a robbery with the most ruthless violence. Adrian Snodgrass was shot. He must have died instantly. Professor Snodgrass and Dr Absolon are both here, and know about it. The police are coming. Indeed, I think I have heard them arriving now.'

'There were some men,' Mrs Anglebury said. 'I saw them. But as for Adrian's death . . .'

'I see.' David Anglebury had squared his shoulders. It was possible to feel that he had also risen on his toes. He might have been a full-back, Appleby thought, prepared to fling himself at the knees, the ankles of a flying three-quarter. 'I don't think this is a thing for my mother to be mixed up in, sir. As a matter of fact, she hasn't been very well recently. May I take her away?'

'I'm afraid not. Not quite yet.'

'Look – is it for you to say? I don't know who you are, or if you are telling the truth, or if you have any authority here at all.' The young man had moved to his mother's side, and was looking dangerous. 'Would you please stand out of the way?'

'I've been a policeman myself, Mr Anglebury. I can still show you a warrant card, for what it's worth. But I assure you that as a simple citizen I'd have a right to detain your mother – having heard from her certain things that I have heard. However, all that's not to the point. Your own good sense will tell you that she ought to stay. And have you beside her.'

'Very well.' A sudden and rather touching bewilderment seemed for the moment to have come uppermost in David Anglebury. It was likely that he was rather far from being particularly clever, and he was confronted by a mature, dispassionate and composed man. 'Only, can we get out of this room? I suppose it was . . . was going to be his. It has been got ready for him. I think it's rather rotten, somehow, our being here at all.'

'Very well, Mr Anglebury.' Appleby had liked this speech by the young man. 'Let us go elsewhere. But I'm afraid there's a good deal that is rotten at Ledward just at present.' And Appleby made a movement almost as if to touch the young man's arm. 'Bring your mother along. And I quite understand about her being not too well.'

Chapter Nine

The police proved to be represented, for the present, simply by the constable from the nearest village, who had arrived in a van, with the local doctor just behind him. Confronted by robbery and murder in high life – or at least in what was by far the most imposing house for many miles around – this officer had the sagacity to perceive that his job was simply to hold the fort until his superiors arrived. He also knew that merit was to be gained by ensuring that, in the interim, he got as much writing as possible into his notebook in an adequately legible hand.

Appleby saw no reason to suppose that the course of justice would be expedited by his at all obtruding himself during this process. He had arrived at Ledward Park under circumstances which no sensible policeman would regard as other than highly suspicious. If, on top of this, he were to produce the outrageous statement that he had lately been running New Scotland Yard, it seemed highly probable that he would be clapped into handcuffs at once.

The local doctor, whose name proved to be Plumridge, was another matter. He was an old rather than merely elderly man, who showed every sign of being able to cope competently with whatever turned up. The dotty Mrs Anglebury, for instance, had turned up; she was presumably one of Dr Plumridge's patients; he was to be detected as considering that a live and disturbed patient was more important than an undisturbable corpse. Not that he hadn't examined the body with care. He didn't seem to feel there was anything all that mysterious about it.

At least the constable appeared to have put Appleby low on his list for interrogation. He had perhaps provisionally concluded that Appleby was a valet or a footman. He was busy at the moment questioning Professor Snodgrass, and was receiving most of the replies from Dr Absolon, who had clearly decided that the distressed uncle of the dead man still needed all the support he could get. Appleby took the opportunity to move over to Plumridge, and murmur that he would appreciate a few words with him in the library. And Plumridge gave him a single swift glance, nodded, and followed him down the quadrant corridor.

'I recognize you,' Plumridge said briskly. 'I've a memory for faces, and even for photographs. Sir John Appleby, isn't it? Has trouble been expected here? Did they persuade you to come along? It can't be. It doesn't make sense.'

'Quite right. It's sheer chance. I walked into this house in the middle of the night, my dear Doctor, and found myself in the middle of all this. Of course, I've no title to ask questions; only to answer them. Presently some police inspector will arrive;

and he'll either be extremely cross that I'm here at all, or take it for granted that I'll clear the affair up for him before breakfast. Either reaction will be vexatious. Still, it's a fair cop.'

'I think you mean that you propose to have a go. But is there all that to have a go at? The affair has had a horrible end, but it doesn't strike me as having any great puzzle-element to it. Thieves panic-stricken when surprised, and ruthless enough and stupid enough to kill somebody.'

'May I meet your question with another one?' They had reached the library door, and Appleby stood aside to let Plumridge enter first. It was as if he were coming to feel himself in at least the temporary position of a host at Ledward. 'You say you have a memory for faces, and you've certainly remembered mine from a magazine or newspaper. What about Adrian Snodgrass? I take it you knew him a long time ago?'

'Dear me, yes. I've been in practice in this corner of England for more than forty years. I knew Adrian as a boy.'

'Very good. And this *is* Adrian?'

'I beg your pardon?' There was astonishment in Plumridge's voice.

'We're talking about faces. There's the remains of a face in this house now.' Appleby said this grimly and without pleasantry. 'Are you quite sure it belongs to somebody whom I gather you're unlikely to have seen over the past ten years or so?'

'Good Lord!' For a moment Plumridge was silent. 'Yes, I think I am.'

'That sounds like only a qualified certainty.'

'I suppose it is, Sir John. But consider how instantly your question has me asking whether I have taken something for granted. Here is this daft annual occasion at Ledward ... By the way, I suppose you know about it?'

'Indeed I do. And it's my growing impression that a great many other people do as well.'

'I'd imagine you to be quite right in that. But here's my point. At dinner tonight, as it happens, I said to my wife, "I wonder whether Adrian Snodgrass will turn up *this* time?" And he *does* turn up. This fellow Leonidas, that's to say, tells me so on the telephone, and that the returned wanderer has been shot while trying to catch some thieves. I arrive and find what we know about. No doubt as to the dead man's identity ever occurs to me. And then you fire that question at me! Naturally, I ask myself whether I can conceivably have been taking something for granted. But I don't think it can be so. Indeed, I wonder how such a conjecture can have come into your head.'

'It was into the vicar's head that it came, as a matter of fact. I think it has gone out of it again now. But he started the hare that this whole business of a long-lost heir being expected home afforded an ideal spring-board, so to speak, for successful imposture. Some pretender has only to persuade the old Professor that he is Adrian, and he's likely to be able to get away with a great deal.'

'It's an ingenious idea. But I doubt, Sir John, whether you are any more disposed to believe in it than I am. Still, we'll *both* have to believe it if one very simple condition holds.'

'What's that?'

'If that dead body proves not to have parted with its appendix. I remember sending Adrian into a nursing-home for an appendicectomy quite thirty years ago. It was uncommonly fashionable at that time. Shall we go back and have a look? I didn't strip the poor chap down to his tummy.'

'Not while that bobby's on the beat, thank you. But if the body *has* had its appendix out . . .'

'That doesn't advance the matter? I quite agree. And I don't suppose Adrian's fingerprints have ever been collected by the police. Or not in this country.'

'Ah?'

'So it may be the dentist or nothing, if a coroner at his inquest gets sceptical. But I increasingly feel, Sir John, that we're on a wild-goose chase. Dash it all, the features aren't all that mutilated. No, it's Adrian. I'm sure of it.'

'What about it being some other Snodgrass, with a close resemblance to the young man you remember?'

'*Is* there such a person?' Plumridge looked puzzled. 'I can't think of one.'

'Of course I haven't a notion, Doctor. It's simply that one has to think of all those possibilities. It's a kind of routine.'

Appleby paused. 'But you said something interesting a moment ago. About fingerprints. "Or not in this country." What do you know about Adrian Snodgrass in other countries? And about the Snodgrasses in general, for that matter? This business of a South American connection for example. I'm quite curious about that.'

'My dear sir, it would take a little leisure to put you at all fully in the picture there.'

'Then why not sit down?' As he spoke Appleby moved towards the fire, which was still by no means extinguished. 'They'll rout us out when they want to.' He paused. 'But what about that Mrs Anglebury? Perhaps you feel you ought to have an eye on her? Particularly if the police . . .'

'Not necessary.' Dr Plumridge had sat down, and was stretching his limbs in frank fatigue. 'I've given her what will by now have knocked her out for some hours. Remarkable privileges, we medical characters have. The police mayn't be pleased, but I simply say my patient's interest comes first. And now, let me tell you anything I usefully can about the person we'll agree to identify with the dead man.'

'Thank you,' Appleby said. 'Thank you very much.'

'I don't know the details,' Plumridge began, 'of what may be called the South American background of these people. But the outline is clear enough. The Snodgrasses have been a good deal intermarried with the Beddoeses, who are another family of the same sort.'

'There was a Beddoes Beddoes who was called the Liberator,' Appleby said.

'Ah, I see you know something about them. I don't think the two families were of the same sort back in the Liberator's time. The Liberator was an adventurer – although he might just as well be called a thug – with nothing much behind him, whereas there had been prosperous Snodgrasses in the Argentine and elsewhere for quite some time before he bobbed up. The man who built this distinctly ambitious house, Augustus Snodgrass, did so largely on the strength of properties in the West Indies; and from there other Snodgrasses had already been taking up land, and so on, on the South American

72

continent for some time. Particularly in Azuera. They seem to have been clever enough, and wealthy enough, to hold their own through a great deal of political turmoil of one sort and another – partly, I believe, on the strength of further judicious marriages which gained them the support of banking interests in the United States.

'The Snodgrasses out there had no doubt become as Spanish as they were English in a good many ways, and I think they prized being accepted by the Blancos, or aristocrats of pure Spanish descent. No doubt they exploited the natives, and the lower classes generally, in a manner merciless enough. But they had their virtues, and I think it would be fair to call them an honourable and high-minded crowd. Certainly they got deeper into politics, and with the best of intentions. The result of that was that their prosperity tended to decline, and their security was threatened in various ways. Roughly speaking, therefore, they came to rely a good deal on their English and American connections. I think their position is something like that today.'

'Great houses like this are contriving to get along in private hands still without a great deal behind them.' Appleby paused. There had been the sound of a car on the drive which probably betokened the arrival of more police. 'Would that be the position of Ledward still?'

'I think not. There's real wealth behind it. And there are other Snodgrasses in England who are people of fortune.'

'It seems to me extraordinary that this unfortunate fellow, Adrian Snodgrass, being actually the proprietor of the place, should have had nothing to do with it for years, nor apparently have benefited from it in any way.'

'Oh, I rather doubt that last proposition. I expect there were bankers upon whom he could draw if he wanted to. Basically it has been a matter of pride, I imagine. Adrian stood by the role his family had allotted him when he was still a younger son.'

'Ah, yes.' Appleby recalled *Who's Who*. '"Eldest surviving son." As a young man, they shipped him off to South America?'

'Just that. He was too wild for the home paddocks. And, in point of family tradition, there was nothing out of the way in it. The branch of the family out there was by way of getting, as I've said, financial backing from Snodgrasses in England. And black sheep would arrive along with the money, as a kind of package deal.'

'A humiliating arrangement, from the young man's point of view.'

'Yes, indeed. But I think the old gentleman here, Beddoes Snodgrass, was the only one to bother his head about that. Adrian must always have been a favourite of his.'

'Is it really a full ten years since he last troubled to turn up and see his uncle?'

'I think of it loosely as that, but if I worked it out I think it might come to only eight. Which was long enough. And it wasn't, incidentally, pure family piety that brought him back to Ledward then. Or I don't think it was. I had a strong impression at the time that he had come here in order to lie low. This will sound melodramatic, I suppose. But I believe there were people who were out for his blood.'

'My dear Doctor!' Under cover of this exclamation of astonishment, Appleby took a sharp look at Plumridge, as if almost suspecting him of some deliberate obfuscation. 'Do you mean political enemies from across the South Atlantic?'

'It sounds absurd, but I'm afraid I do.'

'You saw him at this time you're speaking of? You had some talk with him?'

'Certainly. A good deal of what he said was obscure to me. Adrian might be described as submerged in a world of revolution and counter-revolution of an almost phantasmagoric sort, and he took it for granted that I was as interested and well-informed as he was.'

'It amounted to obsession? He was far from being mentally well-balanced?'

'I think that would have to be called a fair assessment. Adrian had started in the army, you know, and left it pretty promptly under some sort of cloud. And that made him seek, if not exactly martial glory, at least military eminence. So now it was a matter of his wanting to be Commander-in-Chief in Azuera, and probably Minister of War as well. But some rival clique of officers had got their man the job. He was very savage

74

about it; indeed, not altogether sane. He told me several times over that he had in his possession what would cook their bloody goose at any time in their succeeding lives; and that he was capable of playing cat and mouse with them; and biding his time with them, and not striking until he could strike to kill. I'm bound to say I didn't find it all that much worth listening to. And it's probably not worthwhile your hearing about it now. It's past history, after all.'

'I'm grateful to you, all the same.' Appleby found himself taking another sharp look at Plumridge. 'I think this conversation is likely to be interrupted at any moment now. But may I ask you about one other thing? Here is a man of property, shot dead in the very act, so to speak, of turning up to claim it – or, at least, possibly to claim it. So one has to consider . . .'

'But what can this line of thought have to do with more or less petty robbery of pictures, and bits of silver, and high-class knick-knackery of one sort and another?'

'I see that you at least understand what I'm talking about. But the robbery, you know, might be a mere blind. Or what we are confronting may be sheer coincidence. Or not – come to think of it – exactly that, since this particular night may be regarded as offering special scope for more kinds of crime than one. In any case, it's plainly essential to know about who benefits from the death of Adrian Snodgrass – benefits, that is, in the most obvious financial way. Do you know anything about that?'

'Of course not.' Plumridge had admitted a note of impatience into his voice. 'I'm the family doctor, you know, and not the family lawyer. I've no idea what entail – if that's the term – still exists, or what trusts or settlements; or what Adrian's will may prove to say – supposing he has made one, and has in fact owned a substantial power of bequest. Professor Snodgrass might give you a notion – presuming he's willing to be communicative about the matter.'

'Thank you. No doubt he's the proper person to answer the question – and the police who have just arrived are the proper people to ask it. But as for being communicative, Doctor, I judge it improbable that anybody is going to have much choice. Except, conceivably, yourself.'

'My dear Sir John, may I ask what you mean by that?'

'I refer to what's called professional confidence. It's just possible, isn't it, that you may have relevant information – relevant, I mean, strictly to the clearing up of this crime – which you might have to ask yourself questions about in that regard? I believe I could ask you such a question now.' Appleby had risen to his feet, for there were voices at the far end of the quadrant corridor. 'Shall I?'

'Yes, of course. I take your point. But it stands to reason that I shall want to help in every possible way.' Plumridge got up and stood with his back to that now fast-dying fire which had been kindled for Adrian Snodgrass's return to the home of his fathers. 'So go ahead.'

'That young man who came to fetch his mother, and who tells me his name is David Anglebury. Is there any chance that he is Adrian Snodgrass's illegitimate son?'

'I see.' Plumridge's expression had become grave 'Well, it is obvious that there is always a *chance* of such a thing. To put it crudely, any man *may* be the father of any child with whose mother he could conceivably have had sexual relations within a given stretch of time. And you would quickly find, I think, that the possibility applies to Adrian Snodgrass and this particular young man's mother. But that just doesn't begin to be evidence.'

'Of course not.' Appleby was moving towards the door. 'And there's nothing more you can say about it?'

'Not without a little thought.' Plumridge paused on this expression, as if weighing it carefully. And it appeared to satisfy him, because he repeated it at the open door.

'Not without a little thought,' Plumridge said.

Chapter Ten

Detective Inspector Stride seemed a highly conscientious officer; he clearly made it a standing instruction that whenever a murder call came through in the small hours he was to be summoned from his bed. And about Appleby's identity he was as assured as Dr Plumridge had been; some years ago, he explained, he had attended a Crime Squad course at which Sir John gave a much-appreciated lecture. This being so, Stride had decided (perhaps rashly, from the point of view of pure theory) that Appleby was not profitably to be suspected of being either a murderer of wandering heirs or a purloiner of French paintings. And since Appleby *did* happen to have dropped in on Ledward on this rather unusual occasion, Stride opined, he might very well feel like continuing to move around a little. But not – it seemed to be suggested – as an awkwardly high-ranking attaché to Stride's own team. Appleby, finding, at least for the time being, much sense in this, took himself off to another room.

He looked at his watch, and found to his surprise that it was barely past three o'clock. In subjective terms, this impromptu mystery appeared to have been going on for a good deal longer than that. Perhaps the impression was occasioned by his having so far made no real progress in clarifying the affair. There was as much nonsense and inconsequence to it now (he told himself impatiently) as there had ever been. However, at three o'clock, the night, or at least the morning, was still young. There was plenty of time (thus a small seductive voice from the past seemed to murmur in his ear) to tie the whole thing up before breakfast. Or before, at least, the customary hour for that meal. For it seemed improbable, in the present confusion at Ledward, that Leonidas or another would get around to serving coffee and bacon-and-eggs at eight-thirty.

These reflections on the clock led him to recall that there were certain small chronological sequences that needed fixing and clarifying. For instance, there had been the events, or better perhaps, the phenomena that had preluded the actual catastrophe. And these had been introduced by a kind of double prelude. The suggestion of prowlers on the terrace outside the library had been the first of these; and the second had been the lurking presence of Mrs Anglebury (as she had proved to be) at the library door. Between these there had been time for Appleby's first quite substantial colloquy with Professor Snodgrass. After the alarm of the woman in white that colloquy had continued. Then there had been the sounds of Adrian Snod-grass's arrival, and these had prompted Appleby to that abortive withdrawal from Ledward which had led to his unfortunate grapple with Dr Absolon. There had followed a certain amount of palaver before Leonidas had entered with his formal announcement that Mr Snodgrass was in residence. Leonidas had then given his brief account of what might be called Adrian's comportment – and it was hard upon this that the real crush of impressions came. What it wouldn't at all do to muddle was the actual order and succession of these. But Appleby was fairly confident that he hadn't got them wrong.

The darkness had evoked an angry shout, or had at least been instantly followed by one. Then had come running footsteps – the footsteps, surely, of several people pounding along together. And *loud* footsteps. Could they have come from the quadrant corridor immediately beyond the library: the corridor along which he had previously seen Mrs Anglebury disappear? It was difficult to suppose so . . . Appleby frowned. Well, hard upon that had come the sound of the smashed drawing-room window, and *then* the report of the revolver, or whatever the weapon had been. But in between *these* sounds – splintering glass and loud report – there had been the woman's scream. Mrs Anglebury's scream, one had to suppose.

Or had there been a second female prowling Ledward? At present, it was impossible to say. But there was something else that *did*, surely, emerge from this brief analysis. The sequence of sounds he had been recalling lacked – he searched for a word – *lucidity*. There was something odd about them.

These, whether in an intelligible series or not, had been the acoustic effects (or known facts, for that matter) immediately clustered round the main event of the night: namely, Adrian Snodgrass's death. But there was one other, if minor, cluster of events the sequence of which required thinking about. They were the events which had enacted themselves in what might be called the bedroom and dining-room area. As Appleby's mind turned in this direction he found his steps doing so too.

The dining-room was undisturbed. It was in the same disorder, that is to say, as before: the tumbled and broken chair, the shivered wine glass and little puddles of champagne, the ice-bucket that appeared to have been used as a football. Detective officers would presently come to measure and photograph all these appearances with due solemnity. Appleby resisted an inclination to reflect that somebody ought to be keeping an eye on the place meanwhile. At the moment, no doubt, Stride hadn't all that many men to deploy. And there was something much more important to chew on: his own instant sense, as it had been, that the chaos was altogether too much of a good thing, and added cogency to a suspicion which on other grounds it was fairly easy to form. Wasn't there something factitious about the whole affair? Didn't it match the hoary old formula of the inside job disguised as an outside job? Or did it? The fingers of one hand, Appleby told himself, wouldn't serve to enumerate the difficulties in the way of that temptingly simple interpretation.

And now there was again the question of the sequence of certain events – here, in this, as it were, subsidiary area of the mystery. Apart from the library with its welcoming fire, two rooms appeared to have been particularly prepared for the returning Adrian Snodgrass: this dining-room, and the master-bedroom which almost adjoined it. He himself had inspected the bedroom, and had been mildly unnerved, if not by the waiting pyjamas, at least by the waiting hot-water bottle. He had then come into the dining-room, with its answering signs of an expected arrival. And Adrian *had* arrived, and had sat down to a meal. He had rung a bell (somewhat speculatively, that must have been); Leonidas had appeared and explained himself; Leonidas had opened the champagne and at once put another whole bottle on the ice. (Appleby checked on this story now. Yes, sure enough: there was an unbroken bottle that had rolled to a corner of the room.) Adrian had then sent a disrespectfully framed message to his uncle, but before letting Leonidas go had asked him to take a glass of madeira. (Yes, again: two glasses which had been used for madeira stood unbroken on the table.) Leonidas had made his way to the library, and was still giving an account of himself when the house was plunged into darkness.

And now had come the main sequence of events, beginning

with that angry shout. Adrian's shout, it must be supposed: an Adrian who had in the same moment jumped to his feet so violently as to smash a chair, shiver a champagne glass, and send an ice bucket flying. A mere failure of the electricity supply would surely not occasion such a reaction; in the second before darkness fell Adrian must have *seen* something that made him furious. It must have made him furious enough, or alarmed enough, to pick up a poker. *But how had he managed that?*

Anticipating the coming efforts of Stride's assistants, Appleby started searching the dining-room for a burnt match. There just wasn't one. Had Adrian happened to have an electric torch in his pocket? There had been no torch on or near the dead man.

But stick, for the moment, to these two rooms – or rather, now, just to the bedroom, which was so notably a scene of unelucidated events. It had been hard upon the lights going on again (presumably through the instrumentality of Leonidas) that Professor Snodgrass (already much shocked, one must suppose, by the death of his nephew) had made his way there, at Appleby's suggestion, in quest of a sheet with which to cover the body. At this point, Appleby told himself, there had been a time-gap worth remembering. The Professor's mission had taken rather a substantial period in which to fulfil itself. Nor *had* it, in fact, fulfilled itself. The Professor had returned without a sheet, but in a remarkable state of perturbation. Arrived in the bedroom, or at the bedroom door, he had become aware of two or more persons whom he supposed to be thieves and murderers. This had unnerved him to what was really a very surprising extent. He had cowered or hidden for an unspecified number of minutes. And then he had bolted.

What had been happening in the bedroom, or what had then happened there? The next witness was Mrs Anglebury. For some reason (or for no reason at all, perhaps, if she was as crazy as she appeared to be) her wandering progress round the house had brought her there. Like the Professor, she had seen 'some men', and had so little cared for the look of them that she had contrived (in an unexplained fashion) to hide under the bed. It was these men, presumably, who had made an abortive snatch at the mediocre family portrait. In this episode the time-intervals were short, since Appleby had arrived in the bedroom, and rapidly discovered the hidden lady, within minutes of Professor Snodgrass's reappearance in unedifying panic.

Having got so far in this sketchy retrospect, Appleby, who was still standing in the dining-room, decided that the bedroom itself might be worth taking another look at. That portrait of some female Snodgrass of the Victorian era was obscurely coming to him as holding some central significance in the affair. He'd give himself another chance to make reasonable sense of it.

With this object in view, he made his way down the short corridor that brought him to the bedroom door. And here he halted, in a good deal of surprise.

There was a woman in the room. And she was a woman in black.

Chapter Eleven

Women in white – Appleby, who had read much popular fiction in youth, told himself – but *spies* in black. Perhaps this person in black *was* a spy. Perhaps this whole nocturnal episode in which he had involved himself *was* a spy-story. Its general unaccountability would thus be explained.

But now the woman in black was looking at him with extreme disapprobation. Or so, for a moment, he supposed. Then he divined that her disapprobation was by no means concentrated upon himself. She was taking a comprehensively dark view of everything surrounding her.

'And who may *you* be?' the woman in black said.

Instantly upon these words – and because of their accent rather than their burden – Appleby perceived the character of the black garments before him. They didn't belong to a spy in some romance of the past age. They belonged to a contemporary domestic servant. And Appleby was quite good at names.

'Mrs Gathercoal, I think?' he said.

'I'm sure I don't know how you come to know *that*,' the woman said. 'You've never been seen at Ledward before, you haven't. Not that I know, you haven't, have you?'

It was clear to Appleby that Mrs Gathercoal must be a very good cook. Not otherwise could she have overcome educational disabilities inadmissible in good service, and so risen to command the kitchens of Professor Beddoes Snodgrass of Ledward's Old Dower House.

'You're absolutely right,' he said admiringly. 'But I am, as it happens, a guest of the Professor's at the moment. And it won't surprise you that he has mentioned to me the name of his wholly admirable cook.' He paused to mark this going home. 'Did you come over with Leonidas in his car?' he asked.

'Did I not!' It was with vigorous emphasis that Mrs Gathercoal produced this syntactically obscure disclaimer. 'On my own two feet I came. Feeling that an eye ought to be kep' on all this 'ere nonsensicalness.'

'A thoroughly sound feeling.' Appleby had warmed to this. 'It has all been very great nonsense, has it not? Only you haven't yet perhaps heard what it has ended in.'

'Ended in? Would I be surprised! Year after year treating this 'ouse like it was a public – and well after closing time at that.'

'As a matter of fact, my own first notion of Ledward was that it was going to be a public house. But I quite understand what you mean. You disapprove of opening up on the chance of this wandering Mr Adrian choosing to drop in?'

'Arsking for trouble, I call it. Particularly now, with that Leonidas about the place.'

'Mr Leonidas hasn't been at Ledward long?'

'Eighteen months, it might be – but with a lot of come and go as you please. And do I trust him? Like Hitler, I do. Mark you, every butler is entitled to his occasional brandy and cigar. But not to being that idle you'd suppose he was a gentleman.

And wenches, too. They'll be 'is Antilles Heel one day is what I say.'

'Ah, Mrs Gathercoal, women are a terrible risk. I suppose you have been with Professor Snodgrass for some time?'

'Twenty years, I have. And in better 'ouses before that. Seats and residences, I've seen – although I admit its 'aving been in inferior capabilities. Kitchenmaid twice in establishments bigger than Ledward itself. Not that I 'ave anything against the Professor and 'is station in life, I haven't. The old gentry written all over 'im, the Professor has – even although 'e's 'ad to make a living in a University.'

'I'm delighted that you are so well affected towards your employer, Mrs Gathercoal. I don't suppose you ever knew Mr Adrian?'

'Of course I knew 'im!' Mrs Gathercoal was indignant. 'Lived for the outside of a year in this very 'ouse, 'e did, shortly after I came to the Professor. Not that 'e owned it then, not as far as I know. 'Is brother's it was – 'im that lived abroad and died afterwards. That as 'ow I know what nonsensicalness all this is' – Mrs Gathercoal made a gesture comprehending the whole bedroom – 'this and all that in the dining-room too. 'Ot plates and champagne, I arsk you! What a gentleman wants – coming 'ome like that if 'e *does* come 'ome – is a sandwich and a couple of large whisky-and-sodas.'

'Perfectly true, Mrs Gathercoal.' Appleby was regarding the woman in black with genuine respect. 'But perhaps it was different when the Professor was young.'

'This 'ere bedroom, too. A regular museum piece, it is, and Mr Adrian never slep' in it in 'is life. I could take you to 'is proper room, I could, one up from this, which is the one as ought to 'ave been got ready for 'im.'

'Could you, indeed? Do you know, Mrs Gathercoal, I'd be most grateful if you'd do precisely that now. I'd be most interested. Let us go there at once.'

'And just who are you, anyway?' It was with distinguishably diminished challenge that Mrs Gathercoal reiterated this question. Conceivably she had formed the erroneous impression that Appleby, like the Professor, belonged to the old gentry.

'As a matter of fact, Mrs Gathercoal, I am a policeman. In case that puzzles you, perhaps I ought to say rather an upper policeman.'

'Officer class, *I* can see.'

'Well, staff-officer, as a matter of fact. And I'm here – at least I'm remaining here – because a very shocking thing has happened. I must tell you about it, I'm afraid. Mr Adrian Snodgrass *did* come home tonight. But now he's dead. His body's in the drawing-room. Somebody has murdered him.'

'*That* doesn't surprise me, it doesn't!' It was demonstrably without the least striving for effect that the amazing Mrs Gathercoal took this shattering information in her stride. 'A bad 'at, if ever there was one, that young man was. Not that 'e's young now no longer, not if what you say is true. There being neither youth or age, sir, in the 'eavenly mansions – no, nor in the other place either.'

'I imagine your theology to be impeccable. And I must acknowledge that I have myself not formed a favourable impression of Adrian Snodgrass's character. Still, it seems rather hard that he should be done to death hard upon stepping over his ancestral threshold. The matter deserves looking into – wouldn't you agree?'

'That there Leonidas deserves looking into, 'e does. And poking about in too, if you asks me. You'd find evil in that man's guts. Begging your pardon.'

'I intend looking into pretty well everybody, as a matter of fact. And every *where* and every *thing*, while I'm about it.' And Appleby pointed suddenly at the displaced portrait of the Victorian lady. 'Would you, now, know anything about that painting?'

For the first time, Mrs Gathercoal appeared surprised. She walked over to the canvas and stared at it.

'Come off its 'ook, it seems to 'ave done. Mind you, family portraits are said to fall with a crash sometimes when there's ill luck coming to a 'ouse. I've 'eard of that in some very 'igh-class establishments. Would it be that, do you think, sir?'

'I've certainly heard of such phenomena.' Appleby marked with satisfaction that he was now coming in for a properly respectful form of address. 'Although I must admit I hadn't thought of it in this instance. You are not aware of anything special about this picture?'

'Dusted it, from time to time, I 'ave. Not my proper work, not by a long way. But we all give a hand at keeping this place up – being willing to oblige the poor Professor, bless 'im. But it's a poor class of thing, to my eye – me 'aving been in places with Joshuas and the like on the walls.'

'There are some very fine and valuable pictures here at Ledward, Mrs Gathercoal. But your taste is absolutely correct. This isn't one of them. Shall we go up to that bedroom now?'

'Come this way,' Mrs Gathercoal said.

Ledward – Appleby was presently discovering – had what could best be described as a dilatible character. He had earlier concluded (on the basis of some interest in such things) that here was a kind of Kedleston Hall miniaturized. But now the place was taking on the dimensions, if not of a Versailles, at least of a Knole or a Hampton Court. Mrs Gathercoal, having undertaken to conduct him to an apartment modestly described as 'one up from this', had first led him up a service staircase roughly in parallel with the main staircase of the house, and then through a maze of corridors, each sufficiently stately in itself, the rooms opening upon which would have served very adequately to accommodate the general staff of an invading army. Perhaps there *was* an invading army. Almost any number of people, it occurred to Appleby, could have walked into this open house round about midnight, and be still lurking around the place in the interest of no end of nefarious purposes. His progress could not actually have occupied more than two or three minutes. But his sense of disorientation was complete. Were Mrs Gathercoal suddenly to vanish (as so dream-like a character might well do) his hope of returning to the known terrain of that pillared hall before dawn would be slender indeed. But in fact Mrs Gathercoal had now halted before a closed door.

'It's 'ere,' Mrs Gathercoal said.

The oddity of all this was, if anything, enhanced by the blaze of light in which every corner of the house was still bathed. It had occurred to nobody to moderate or mitigate the pervasive illumination which Professor Snodgrass had deemed it proper to create for the reception of the wandering heir. Appleby glanced to right and left. This particular corridor had been judged suitable for the exhibition, or storage, of rather a large collection of medieval armour. It hung on the walls with the suggestion of a kitchen lavishly equipped with outlandish utensils in some sort of stainless steel; it perched on stands to the creating of a threatening appearance of ranked and patient flunkeys stricken into a robot-like cohort of metallic presences. The family of Snodgrass had not, it was to be presumed, flourished in great station when such accoutrements were of much practical utility. These vistas of junk witnessed only to the ineradicable acquisitiveness of the human species. Snodgrasses had been for quite some time, of course, followers of the profession of arms. Busbies, bearskins, and Balaclava helmets would have been entirely in order, and one might even have expected outlandish uniforms from the fringes of civilization such as the little Adrian was dressed up in for the purposes of the photograph now to be seen in the library downstairs. But there was something disturbing in this entirely bogus suggestion of ancestral activity on the fields of Poictiers and Agincourt.

Reflections of this sort (not at all relevant to the matter in hand) were cut abruptly short. Mrs Gathercoal had opened the door of Adrian Snodgrass's authentic bedroom.

This was the moment – as it transpired – when the less boring part of Sir John Appleby's night out began.

There were certainly two men – and Appleby wasn't at all sure that he hadn't glimpsed a third. They were patently not policemen – although it might certainly be termed investigation that they seemed to be about. There was a desk in a window embrasure with half its drawers pulled out – beginning (Appleby instantly recognized the professional touch) from the bottom and not from the top. On the farther wall, beyond a simple bed, hung what appeared to be a dim and darkened portrait of a Tudor lady. And one of the men was in the act of lifting it from its hook.

'You can stop all that,' Appleby said – and heard his own

voice come to him with the calm authority of years at this sort of thing. 'The police are here, and you're through.'

This admirable speech certainly produced an instant effect – but not quite the effect that was to be desired. Instantly and entirely, darkness fell. The lights in this bedroom, it had to be supposed, could be controlled from a farther door, and one of the intruders had made a very successful dash to the switch. There was still, indeed, a beam of light from the corridor behind Appleby and Mrs Gathercoal. But it was a moment before this effectively assisted sight. And this moment was filled by the sound of flying feet – a sound, Appleby told himself, which was becoming something like the *leit-motif* of this perplexing nocturnal occasion. This time, they made it clear that the marauders were by no means trapped. In a house like this, rooms still communicated with rooms which communicated with yet farther rooms in quasi-regal fashion. And through this sort of vista the footsteps were fading fast.

'Mrs Gathercoal, go downstairs to the drawing-room and send up the police.' Appleby shouted this as he ran. A proper professional phlegm had suddenly deserted him. He'd had enough. He was very angry indeed. If he could come within reach of one of these rascals, he'd bring him down with a crash he wouldn't quickly forget.

This resolution, perhaps injudicious in an elderly man whose occupation had been many years of a sedentary sort, was at least spirited and indeed inspiriting. Appleby made surprising speed. Even so, he saw that any success attending his pursuit must depend on two factors: the promptness with which he was backed up by Stride and his men, and the extent to which the lay-out of the house was as unfamiliar to his quarry as it was to himself. In this second regard he might, indeed, hold an advantage. The evidence, although painfully contradictory and obscure so far, did point to the possibility that these noisy and blundering people were not up to their job – whatever that job might prove to be. They knew how to rifle a desk. But, facing the problem of what looked like a rummage through Ledward, it seemed conceivable that they had failed to do adequate home-work in the way of casing the joint first. Very full ground-plans and elevations of a notable house like this could certainly be turned up with only a little informed research among books on English architecture. If they hadn't thought of this then Appleby, knowing about such places in a general way, might have the edge on them. Knowing, for example, that he was now on the first floor of the main building, and that the outer wall was on his right, he knew that eventually there must be a left turn which would prove to be a cul-de-sac. Stateliness has to be paid for by inconvenience: the hall and saloon between them, thrusting up the full height of the building from façade to façade, must cut the entire formidable structure into two symmetrical and self-contained halves, between which the only communication would be at basement level or through the hall or saloon themselves. It might be possible to corner a fellow who didn't realize that.

Appleby's feet rang on marble. He was in a bath-room which had been shoved in between two bedrooms and was shared by each. You had to reckon, of course, with all sorts of odd structural alterations and adaptations in a place of this sort. He could still hear footsteps – and now suddenly there was the sound of a door thrown violently open and then slammed shut. It was followed, more faintly, by the suggestion of a second door being treated in the same way. Some idea of thus impeding a pursuer's progress must be behind this. Sure enough, before him in the second bedroom was a closed door. Flinging it open, he judged it odd that the fugitives, so far, hadn't thought to flick at ...

But this time, they had. Once more, Appleby was staring into darkness.

Or rather, once more into *near* darkness. There was plenty of light behind him – and a pretty target he must be, silhouetted against it. He took a swift sideways step, feeling for a light-switch as he did so. He found it at once, and what he had already distinguished as a small boudoir-like apartment sprang into full visibility. The hold-up had hardly been worth contriving. But now he saw that the system of intercommunicating rooms had come to an end. The only other door was on the left, and must give on the corridor. He crossed to it, and threw it open. The corridor, of course, ran in both directions. At any point in this chase so far, one or more of the fugitives might have bolted into it and doubled back. Only his ear had assured him that there was at least one man ahead of him still. The whole corridor lay in a subdued but adequate light. The switches here must have eluded any hasty search for them. There was nobody to be seen. But there *were* faint sounds, and they still came from the direction in which he had been going. But what appeared to be the end of the corridor was now only a little way in front of him. He must be coming to one of the corners of the main building.

Only he wasn't. The appearance before him was a consequence of some quirky piece of reconstruction. The breadth of the corridor had been taken into a room – which thus merely interrupted the run of it. Appleby swung into this room. It brought him into the presence of the enemy. And not of one enemy, or of two enemies or three. If he had earlier entertained the fancy that Ledward could absorb a whole army – well, here was precisely that.

It was decidedly disconcerting thus to come suddenly upon scores of ruffians – and the more so because all of them appeared to be in violent movement. Only, as if through some benevolent interposition of Providence, there were now scores of Applebys as well. The Applebys were all standing stockstill, and plainly engaged in thinking something out. This process didn't take long. Nothing miraculous, or even magical, had occurred. It was simply that some deceased Snodgrass had taken it into his head to construct a many-sided room, probably an octagon, and to line it with enormous looking-glasses.

The poet speaks of multiplying variety in a wilderness of mirrors – no doubt with some implication of arcane erotic satisfactions. Perhaps the departed Snodgrass had engaged here in high jinks with what Dr Absolon would call Paphian girls. Perhaps he had merely used the place's optical profusion to come to nice decisions on the bow of a tie-wig, the snug fit of a pair of breeches, or the cut of a broad-skirted coat. Or perhaps the chamber had been conceived for practising fencing, or for drill which should bring to near perfection the elegant evolutions of the minuet or the gavotte. None of these pleasures, whether censurable or innocent, was in question now. What the single person in the room, other than Appleby himself, was trying to do was simply to find a way out. The door through which Appleby had come, and which he now closed rapidly behind him, was itself a seemingly unframed mirror. Presumably there was another such, leading to the farther corridor. But the fellow was quite failing to find it. He was pretty well in the bag. There was, indeed, a certain element of visual confusion in the situation, and some concentration would be required if a successful dive were to be made at substance rather than shadow. But Appleby was perfectly capable of this. His only doubt was as to whether he should address any remark to his victim before falling upon him. He decided to accomplish all in a grim silence. His last audible address to the miscreants against whom he was pitted had not produced any very satisfactory result.

Appleby tensed his muscles and marked his man.

Chapter Twelve

Unfortunately this empty room (for it was totally devoid of furniture: a circumstance curiously enhancing, through the absence of any immobile object, its kaleidoscopic effect) had not lately received any great attention from those members of Professor Beddoes Snodgrass's domestic staff whose additional task it was to devote a certain amount of spit-and-polish to Ledward Park. The mirrors, indeed, were unclouded, and the lighting was undimmed. But there was a good deal of dust.

This might have meant no more than the prospect of a rather grubby rough-and-tumble on the floor. As it happened, however, some sudden movement on the part of Appleby's adversary – a swift side-step, perhaps, to avoid being pounced upon – had the consequence of kicking a spurt of dust into Appleby's face. And not only dust. There was an element of what could only be called grit involved. Otherwise, Appleby would not have found himself, at least for certain vital moments, virtually blinded in one eye. He was thus reduced, during a most critical posture of the affair, to reliance upon monocular vision only. In other words, he abruptly lost his sense of the 3D world. He had been transported, as it were, to Flatland, where an image in a mirror is indistinguishable from the solid object which occasions it.

This state of affairs ought to have redounded to the immediate advantage of the adversary. That it did not, in fact, appear to do so was a circumstance that would have puzzled an observing psychologist. Such a one (if he may be imagined as having contrived our spectacle by way of an experimental situation) would have been astounded to perceive both Appleby and his enemy simultaneously reduced to the condition of two sadly over-bewildered Pavlovian dogs. Both men dived hither and thither as if in a kind of maniacal ballet: the one seeking to grasp what eluded him except as a slippery surface of silvered glass; the other dodging arms which were in fact powerless to extend themselves beyond the profoundly mysterious dimension which a mirror constitutes. It was evident that the intruder had become, for the nonce, as one-eyed as Appleby.

But this situation was insusceptible of indefinite continuance – if only because of the frangible quality of what encapsulated the contestants. As they banged about and threshed around, the glass began to give up. It cracked, it shivered, it fell out first in small bits and then in large ones. Mingled with this treacherous debris, this razor-sharp detritus, there was presently a certain amount of blood. The eventual consequence might have been lethal, since in all this shattered looking-glass there was sufficient weaponry to sliver and shred whole platoons of cops and robbers. As it happened, however, Appleby, who was reduced to hitting out somewhat wildly at anything which seemed to suggest the quality of hittability, presently landed a blow to such effect that his enemy was sent hurtling backwards – and actually with the force of a projectile through the very door he had been seeking in vain when Appleby came upon him. Appleby was left staring at the shattered door; and at his elusive quarry, thus lucklessly liberated, picking himself up and once more bolting down the corridor.

With all the pertinacity of a Hound of the Baskervilles (or of Heaven, although the comparison is a profane one), Appleby took one deep breath, and followed. He thought

poorly of the local police. Even if Mrs Gathercoal had somehow failed of her mission, the rumpus created by the breaking
up of this beastly room must surely have carried to the farthest
limits even of this enormous house. But perhaps the acoustics
of the affair had been confusing, and the forces of the law had
gone pounding off to the other side of the mansion. In any
case, Appleby himself wasn't going to let go now. He didn't
believe the fugitive was in any better shape than he himself
was. Another good swipe at him, and it would only remain to
lock him up.

In this belligerent mood, he pounded on. His quarry was
still in view, and now the end of the corridor was really in sight.
The pursuit had been down the whole depth of the house. If,
at the end of the immediate vista, the fellow turned left, it
would be down another and much shorter corridor, or through
a small suite of rooms, which would end in the blank wall supporting the dome of the saloon. What else could he do? In each
of the four angles of the main building, Appleby guessed,
there would be a small staircase. This would go up to another
bedroom floor (it was only the main building that had three
storeys), and down to the quadrant corridor curving away to
one of the four wings, or pavilions, of the edifice. If there *were*
four wings. For he was certain of the existence of only two:
the kitchen wing, and the wing which included the library.
Quite often one found that these great houses had never been
quite completed on the plan proposed, and that their remorse-
lessly projected double-axis symmetry had thus never fully
realized itself. In any case, such a staircase would certainly
continue down to the basement – which would probably be a
maze of low vaulted chambers in which hide-and-seek could
be played till the cows came home. Whether the chap went
up or down, Appleby's best chance of grabbing him would be
before he got clear of the staircase itself.

Meanwhile, what had happened to the other members of
this gang? There had certainly been one other man in Adrian
Snodgrass's authentic bedroom when he and Mrs Gathercoal
had arrived there; and he was still inclined to the opinion that
there had actually been three. So one man – or two men – had
presumably doubled back on his tracks, and succeeded in get-

ting away. But was getting away really, as yet, in these people's plans? Here, as everywhere else, there was a conflict of evidence. The state of the drawing-room window seemed to attest one precipitate withdrawal when surprised; there had been a similar retreat from the bedroom downstairs – as later from the other one. But Adrian Snodgrass had been murdered; whereas in these subsequent episodes there had been flight without violence – except, of course, that this present fleeing man had resisted when Appleby had actually made to apprehend him. How far would these people (with their odd interest in female portraiture) again go in an extremity? Appleby had a feeling that the man now ahead of him was not armed. But what about the other, or the others? Might accomplices of this fellow actually be shadowing him now, prepared for desperate measures if they were required? That one would answer itself, he told himself grimly, if and when he really did make a capture.

And now Appleby was gaining ground. If the man turned right, and if the expected staircase was in fact there, he would be close enough on his heels to know for certain whether he had gone up or down. There was a big armoire against the right-hand wall almost at the end of the corridor, and suddenly the man had dodged behind it. But then for a second he was visible again. Or rather, his head and shoulders were. A staircase there certainly was, and the fellow was plunging down it.

Appleby put on speed. He had a notion that his years were best accommodated to the flat, and that if he didn't want to break his neck he had better resign himself to falling back a bit on the stairs. But when he got to them he changed his mind. Prudence, after all, was a poor sort of notion in a situation like this. It was a spiral staircase, and fairly easy. At least it wouldn't be like the mediaeval variety of the same thing, with here and there a cunningly contrived irregular tread to stumble anybody unfamiliar with it. Thus encouraged, he arrived at its foot – or rather at the point where it reached the ground-floor – before the fugitive was half-way along the corridor.

For there *was* a corridor: another of those curving affairs reaching out to a more or less independent wing. This wing, he guessed, must be diagonal to the private wing. He wondered what on earth the most expansive Snodgrasses had found to do with yet another structure which would have made a very tolerable gentleman's residence in itself. Perhaps he'd find a picture gallery, or a music gallery, or both. Or perhaps just emptiness.

The man had wheeled right and vanished. It was now or never, Appleby told himself, and wheeled right too. There was only a faint light in this unexplored quarter of Ledward. But there was a very strong smell. He passed an arched doorway giving upon some apparently vaulted chamber of indistinguishable character; and then the light had grown yet dimmer and the smell had increased. He was in a greenhouse. But it was a greenhouse of gigantic proportions. As his eyes grew accustomed to the gloom, he saw that it sheltered whole trees. And they were tropical trees: writhing, with unnaturally large and waxen foliage, dropping thick tendrils like hangman's ropes from their upper branches, showing here and there enormous red blossoms, like gouts of blood on wounded dinosaurs. Appleby found that he didn't like them, or the rank warm odour of rotting vegetation upon which they seemed to batten, at all. Nor did he much fancy the place as terrain in which to continue to hunt a desperate man. Whether the fellow had knowingly sought this particular sancturary or not, he had found a quite wonderful lurking place. For in addition to the displeasing trees there was any amount of jungle-like undergrowth. Some of it looked, indeed, discouragingly prickly. But there were thickets of fern and bamboo and luxuriant grasses within which one could have hidden a whole phalanx of fugitives.

It was uncommonly hot and sticky. From somewhere came an alarming hissing sound, so that Appleby for a moment expected the appearance of fauna among the flora in the form of snakes and serpents hastening forward to enfold him in their mortal coils. Then he realized that what he was hearing was nothing more noxious than a gentle escape of steam through some defective joint or valve. Keeping up Ledward Park for a returning Adrian must include the weird extravagance of maintaining this enormous conservatory at a tropical heat. The absurdity of this, when perceived, at once conditioned Appleby's expectation of what might turn up in the place. Instead of veritable pythons, boa constrictors, and rattlesnakes (supplied, conceivably, by the South American connections of the Snodgrasses), he found himself thinking of those comical wild beasts – amiable tigers, beaming lions, and anatomically improbable elephants – to be encountered in mediaeval bestiaries, or later in the agreeable jungle canvases of the *douanier* Rousseau. This sort of reflection (not at all pertinent to the matter on hand) perhaps hinted that he was growing tired, or even sleepy – which, at four o'clock in the morning, would have been reasonable enough. But in fact his senses were still very sufficiently alert, and they abruptly apprised him of something now. Apart from the escaping steam (which now suggested itself as coming from a prehistoric monster so vast that its last breath, after being worsted in mortal combat, could be relied upon to last for something over an hour), there wasn't a sound. The vegetation, if at deadly grips with itself in the manner that exotic writers of equatorial romance would approve, was getting on with the job of self-strangulation quite silently. There wasn't so much as the sound of a prickly pear quietly puncturing a custard apple. But there *was* a sound from the single other chamber into which this particular wing appeared to be divided. It was the sound of a sharp involuntary cough.

Not for the first time that night, Appleby didn't waste a moment. It was probable that the ruffian would realize he had betrayed himself, and that he would now make a dash for some door or window through which he could gain the final freedom of the park. But there was a possibility of intercepting him still. So Appleby doubled out of the hot-house (not without the perception that there was sweat in his eyes and that his shirt was wringing wet) and made for what had been no more than the hastily glimpsed chamber next door. He wondered why he had dashed past it as he had done. It could only be because he had received the impression that the fleeing man had done so before him. The trouble was the very low lighting in this part of Ledward. Here, indeed, through the arched portal which he had now gained, was what the poet Milton might call a dim religious light.

Precisely that. For he was on the threshold of a private chapel.

In addition to being a Justice of the Peace (and a Companion of the Most Distinguished Order of St Michael and St George), Sir John Appleby was a churchwarden. It offended him that a miscreant whom there was the strongest reason to believe implicated in a singularly brutal murder should thus have taken sanctuary upon what was undoubtedly consecrated ground. A private chapel is an increasingly uncommon, and therefore all the more edifying, adjunct of a country seat; this private chapel, even in the near obscurity in which it was at present shrouded, showed as being (like the greenhouse) more or less in use; it had been thus maintained by the piety of Professor Snodgrass (it was to be supposed) for the purpose of assisting in his devotions the wandering heir of Ledward when he should eventually choose to turn up. A somewhat sanguine view of his nephew's spiritual state might have been involved. Nevertheless the impulse was to be respected, and the present violation of the place ought to be ended with all speed. Appleby strode into the chapel.

At least it wasn't a little hall of mirrors, liable to occasion the sort of buffoonery associated with a fun fair. There would be one identifiable rascal, and Appleby was going to nail him. *And there he was.* There he was, immediately in front of the altar – a circumstance by which Appleby found his displeasure markedly increased. And now, apparently most justly alarmed, the man had bobbed down, as if to avoid observation, upon his knees. Appleby hurled himself forward to the tackle he had been dreaming of for quite some time. There was a brief and indecent confusion of thudding bodies and flailing limbs. And then a familiar voice spoke.

'My dear Sir John,' Dr Absolon said a little breathlessly, 'are these recurrent demonstrations really necessary?'

'I must repeat that I'm extremely sorry,' Appleby was saying a minute later. 'But you seemed to dodge, you know. To take evasive action. To attempt to drop out of sight.'

'It may appear odd to you, or even suspicious, but the simple fact is that I came here to pray. After what has happened at Ledward tonight it appeared the reasonable thing to do. From my point of view, that is to say.'

'Yes, of course. I don't . . .'

'And it does happen that, for the purposes of prayer, a certain bodily posture is prescribed. It has been usual for really quite a long time. We get on our knees. You may have seen it in quaint old pictures.'

'Yes, of course.' It interested Appleby that the mild Dr Absolon was, for the moment, an angry man, and one with a considerable gift for simple sarcasm. 'I was extremely precipitate. But, you see, I've been chasing somebody all over this damned house. I beg your pardon. Over this house. He's given me the slip, all right. And I copped you instead. For the second time, I agree. Which does make it peculiarly aggravating. I hope you're not hurt?'

'My dear Appleby, I am little, if at all, older than you are – and in tolerably good condition. Of course I'm not hurt. The question is, where do we go from here?'

'Nowhere at all, at the moment. By which I mean that I'd greatly appreciate a little further conversation with you – and away from all those policemen. If you're sufficiently magnanimous, that's to say, not to want to call them in yourself, and have me locked up as a dangerously violent person. This isn't a bad place for talk. I certainly prefer it to the crazy structure next door.'

'I agree that we are quite comfortable.'

The two men were in fact now sitting on the steps of the altar, and facing each other slant-wise. It was rather like the Pope and the Archbishop of Canterbury (Appleby thought frivolously) in solemn colloquy in the Sistine Chapel.

'You know,' Appleby said conversationally, 'for some time this affair was developing much in the manner of one of those boring modern plays that get along with no more than three or four characters all the way through. But the cast has been filling out, I'm glad to say. Those prowling predators, for example, adept at making improbable noises off-stage. They really exist. Snodgrass saw them. That unfortunate Mrs Anglebury saw them. A new chum of mine, Mrs Gathercoal, has seen them. And now . . .'

'Mrs Gathercoal? You don't mean to say she's turned up?'

'She has, indeed. And shares my opinion of this whole damned . . . I beg your pardon again. Of this whole affair. She disapproves of it strongly.'

'We must all do that.' Rather unfairly in view of the irony in which he had lately indulged on the subject of Appleby's nescience in the matter of prayer, Absolon gave this a tone of mild rebuke. 'But you were saying . . .?'

'That *I've* seen them too. Which is the important thing. That's to say, from my point of view.'

'Quite so.' The vicar had acknowledged this deft echo with a cheerful nod. 'The only person you can trust not to be a damned liar – I beg your pardon, Appleby: a liar – is Sir John Appleby, eh?'

'Decidedly so. It's a cardinal principle in detective investigation.'

'And you're giving me an opportunity to spin you a few more obfuscating stories now?'

'Nothing of the kind, sir.' Appleby had turned serious. 'But everybody concerned in this wretched business may be inclined to one or another sort of reticence. Dr Plumridge, for example. There are things he might feel under a professional obligation not to air.'

'Yes, indeed. And, on a different plane, you may feel it may be the same with me. I do hear confessions, as a matter of fact – although I don't judge it necessary to shut myself up in a little box to do so.'

'The box is an irrelevance.'

'Yes.' Absolon was now as serious as Appleby. 'But I can tell you that nothing has ever come to me from this house, or from anybody connected with it, by way of what may be called ghostly confidence.'

'Not even from Mrs Anglebury, Vicar? She strikes me as the sort of woman . . .'

'I understand you perfectly. She is a little mad, and may therefore be vulnerable to priestcraft.'

'That's most unfair. You're building up a false picture of me as a scoffer.' Appleby was aware of himself as coming, most unprofessionally in the light of the present mysterious circumstances, simply to like Dr Absolon. 'But she obviously needs a good deal of support, and her son has not always been old enough to give it to her. You may feel that, at some time or other, you have received confidences from her, not in any formal sense in your clerical character.'

'Quasi-formal, so to speak. But no. I have occasionally indulged in conjectures about her. In the light of what confronts us, they're at your service, should they be of the slightest use to you.'

'Is she a magistrate?'

'Of course not!' There was simple astonishment in Absolon's voice. 'She is a person of some position in this part of the world. But nobody would dream of shoving her on a bench.'

'Then she's a quite reckless liar. And she says it was she who killed Adrian Snodgrass.'

'She still may have done.'

'Yes, indeed.' Dr Absolon, Appleby saw, was quite reasonably tough. 'And, no doubt, she may be a wronged woman – even although she is quite flamboyantly posturing as one.'

'For what it's worth, Sir John, I haven't a doubt of her being a wronged woman. And my heart goes out to wronged women. Nevertheless, we do have to get at the truth.'

'She was this brutally murdered man's mistress long ago?'

'In my opinion, yes.'

'And the young man going by the name of David Anglebury is their son?'

'You have only to look at the boy.'

'And the boy has only to look at himself in his shaving mirror?'

'No, no – one can't say that. When did he last, or ever, set eyes on Adrian? I just don't know.' The vicar was silent for a moment. 'Deep waters,' he said soberly.

There was a pause in this strange discussion. And no sound from an outer world disturbed it. Whatever of industrious investigation was going on in Ledward, no murmur of it reached this small asylum.

'The first thing anybody would want to know,' Appleby resumed presently, 'I just haven't been able to come by. I ask Snodgrass, and we are interrupted, or in some way distracted. I ask Plumridge, and he tells me he isn't the family lawyer. No more are you. But consider. Adrian may be dead, for he hasn't been heard of for years. He turns up, presumably to claim his inheritance, which is a very rich one. And somebody promptly kills him, amid a great deal of obfuscation. Your own word, Vicar. As the journalists say – or used to say – *qui bono*? Who inherits? It's the first thing to ask,' Appleby paused. 'I suppose there is, or has been, a Mr Anglebury? A Mr Anglebury Senior, that's to say.'

'Dear me, yes. I knew him. He died a great many years ago.'

'And a great many things appear to have happened a great many years ago. I have an increasing sense that, in this business, the dickens of a number of relevant facts lie in hiding-places much more than ten years deep. And I confess to you that I've promised myself to flush them out before breakfast-time.'

'A bold speech, Sir John. By the way, I find myself to have addressed you several times as Appleby. We seem to have known each other for quite a long time. This night is taking on very odd dimensions, wouldn't you say?'

'Yes – but, once more, we're drifting away from what I want to know. There was somebody called Anglebury, who presumably acknowledged young David as his son. And who presumably believed himself to be this demented – or at least hysterical – woman's legal husband. Is it possible that he was mistaken, or at least content that he should be supposed so? Was that marriage, in fact, a bigamous one? Can she have been already married to David's true father? In other words, is David Anglebury the true heir?'

There was another silence. This time, it was a long one.

'Deep waters, Appleby. Deep waters, indeed.'

'No doubt.' This sage reiteration had brought a hint of impatience into Appleby's voice. 'But there must be *some* firm ground in this particular area we're considering. Young Mr

Anglebury is at least not – so to speak – heir apparent. Adrian's dead. And *somebody* – somebody I don't seem as much as to have heard of – owns this place now. Or will own it, at least, as soon as the lawyers have done their stuff, and collected their fees. Who? Can it possibly be the old Professor?'

'I hardly suppose it usual to inherit from a nephew, unless by way of bequest. If Adrian had Ledward in his gift, so to speak, and thought it sensible to leave it to somebody in extreme old age, then it might no doubt work out that way. There's a sense in which Beddoes Snodgrass would deserve the heritage. It has meant much to him. But I don't know that the dead man – although one ought not to speak other than charitably of him – was one markedly aware of the finer considerations.'

'I'd somehow suppose not.' Appleby had found this temperate speech depressing. 'But, you know, it's my point that there must be a legal next of kin to Adrian: somebody who will inherit if he has died intestate, or who would inherit in any case, because of some fashion in which the property is settled. But I just don't know . . .'

The rest of this sentence, if completed, went unheard by Dr Absolon. For the silence of Ledward had suddenly been shattered by a tremendous explosion.

Chapter Thirteen

This time, Stride and his men were very promptly alerted, and it was on their way to the scene of this fresh outrage that they came upon Mrs Gathercoal. She had been chloroformed, bound, and gagged with brisk effectiveness. Which accounted for her failure to perform her late mission.

Adrian Snodgrass's bedroom – his authentic bedroom – was in poor shape. The blast had knocked it around quite strikingly. Even the portrait of the Tudor lady had been damaged, although it had actually been removed (with an odd solicitousness) to the farther end of the room. Set into the wall where it had hung was a small safe – or rather the remains of a small safe after a wholly disproportionate blasting operation had been performed on it. It was empty except for a small twist of metal which had once been a paper-clip.

'Not nearly so neat,' Stride said dispassionately, 'as the job on the Professor's unfortunate cook. That was professional, and this is amateur. They can't have been by the same hand. Or is that jumping to a conclusion? Drugging and kidnapping and what-not may be in their regular way of business, but this is their first shot at blowing a safe. Does it occur to you, sir, that the safe now looks rather like Adrian Snodgrass's face?'

'Well, I can't say that it *had*.' Appleby was startled by this command of the macabre in a stolid police-officer. 'But I see what you mean. The same sort of excessive head-on effect. An overplus of straight brutality. Murder and robbery, and the same criminal putting his signature to both crimes ... I wonder.'

'It's fairly easy to see what happened. In this particular area of our inquiry, I mean.' Stride gestured round the devastated bedroom. 'They got the rooms wrong at first, and consequently the pictures. Hence the monkeying with the one in the room that had been got ready for Adrian Snodgrass. They had 'bedroom" and "woman's portrait", you might say, as clues; but beyond that, their intelligence wasn't precise enough. Eventually, after some pretty cool continuing to lurk around this uncommonly commodious house, they got up here; and they were just going to look behind *this* picture when you and Mrs Gathercoal interrupted them. They must have numbered at least three, if you ask me, and when they bolted two of them must have got into the corridor and doubled back pretty quick. They were in time to intercept and deal with Mrs Gathercoal before returning here and preparing to blow the safe more or less at leisure. For meantime, you see, the third was leading you a pretty dance, sir. A decoy, he might be called.' There was a mild and inoffensive note of professional malice in Stride's offering this sally. 'And then, of course, down there in the chapel, you put in a little time having a chat with the vicar. Giving him the sense, perhaps, of what they call assisting the police with their inquiries.'

102

'No doubt, Inspector.' Appleby thought it unnecessary to appear amused. 'And now that you have refreshed us with wit, we may perhaps proceed to a sober consideration of the matter. I would value your opinion on the Campagna with Banditti.'

'On the what?'

'The painting by Claude, which was over the chimney-piece in the drawing-room. Were they looking for a safe behind that? I hardly think so. It hasn't been displaced; it has been removed. Have you any notion of its approximate value?'

'Enormous, no doubt, on a legitimate market. I'm told there's ceasing to be any sense in such things. Pretty high, even on a black market. And if it's heavily insured, and the insurers were willing to play, worth a great deal simply on a ransom basis.'

'Exactly. I see you have a very good sense of such things. The Claude would be far more valuable than anything likely to be stored in this safe.'

'Family jewellery?'

'I doubt it. Not if Ledward's affairs are administered in any sensible fashion. Really valuable jewellery, if there is no present use for it, is nearly always stored in banks or strongrooms, where insurance costs very much less than in a vulnerable safe like this.'

'Bank-notes of high denomination?'

'Perhaps. But, again, nobody is going to tuck away really large sums in that way for years on end. Think of inflation. Real value would be dropping year by year. Does it occur to you, Inspector, that this safe may have contained objects of interest rather than objects of value?'

'I don't know that I quite follow you, sir.'

'Well, say a family tree. Or a birth certificate, or marriage lines, or a diary. There are all sorts of possibilities.'

'I have found that to be commonly the case, sir, when one is completely at sea before a mystery.'

'Perfectly true, and the thought is a sobering one. But I must not further detain you. Unless, Inspector, I can help you in any way.'

103

'Well, there is one matter, Sir John. Professor Snodgrass doesn't seem able to give much of a description of the men he came upon in the downstairs bedroom – if that *is* where he came upon them – and the lady, Mrs Anglebury, has been given something by Dr Plumridge that has fairly knocked her out. But what about yourself, Sir John? You're the trained man, if I may put it that way, who had a sight of them.'

'Perfectly true. But I can only speak for one of them. Although, mark you, I glimpsed him in about a thousand different aspects in those damned mirrors. Shall I tell you how he struck me, Inspector?' And Appleby looked solemnly at Stride. 'As a sinister foreigner. Just that.'

'I see.' Stride looked doubtful. 'Might I ask why sinister?'

'He was dark, my dear fellow. What is called swarthy. And with a villainous-looking drooping moustache.'

'That's something to go on.' Stride had taken this frivolity very well. 'And you could identify him?'

'Parade him, Inspector, and I'll promise to walk srtaight up to him.'

'Which is a great deal more. Would you say, sir, that, having cracked this safe, they'd brought off their trick, and had nothing more to do than to beat it?'

'It's a grim conclusion. But I confess to seeing it very much like that. Is Mrs Gathercoal all right? I rather took to her.'

'She has come to no harm at all. But she might be a deep one, if you ask me.'

'Indeed? It's an interesting point of view. The confederate who is knocked out and tied up? I've come across it, I confess. And there's a good deal more that one has a sense of having come across. The vicar, by the way, seemed to have the same feeling at one point. He kept on advancing ingenious theories out of a wide reading in detective stories. But now I think he's sobered up.'

'Ah, drink!' Detective Inspector Stride revealed himself as being of somewhat literal mind. 'That's something one always has to think about. There seems to have been a lot of port drunk in that library.'

'Indeed, yes. I myself was plied with it.'

'And that champagne.' Stride had tactfully ignored Appleby's comment. 'Apart from a glass or thereabout that got spilt, the dead man seems to have drunk a bottle of it. And after some sherry to begin with.'

'Madeira.'

'And, what's more, he seems to have intended to go on to a second bottle.'

'In the company of his uncle, perhaps. But I agree that in his last moments Adrian may not have been too clear in his head. He seems to have been resolved to make his home-coming a convivial occasion. He took a glass of the madeira with his uncle's butler. By the way, I suppose that fellow has returned to Ledward?'

'Leonidas? He came back, all right. He and the Professor have been having a word together in the hall, sitting on one of those marble benches. Chilly things. Bad for the backside, if you ask me. None too pleased with each other either, by the look of them.'

'The Professor and Leonidas? I'd be on the Professor's side, I think. There's a covert insolence about that fellow I don't at all like. If he were my employee, I doubt whether he'd long survive unfired. But that's neither here nor there. And Professor Snodgrass, incidentally, is the person I now rather want to talk to again. If you approve, that is, Inspector. This is your case.'

'You're very welcome, I'm sure.' Stride was showing signs of sinking into gloom. 'There's no sense to be got out of that old gentleman at present. None at all. Of course, we must remember he has had a great shock.'

'So he has. Only – do you know? – I'm not as confident as I'd like to be about just what that great shock was.'

'I'd like to be confident of anything at all,' Stride said with sudden savagery, 'in this damned case.'

But confidence was a quality which appeared to have returned to Professor Snodgrass. He was still perched, indeed, on one of those marble benches which Stride had aspersed as fundamentally unsound. But it was with an air of relaxation that made itself felt at once. Both the horror of his nephew's death and the nasty jar of his sudden glimpse of a gang of murderers seemed to have faded on him; he was watching a good deal of coming and going on the part of the constabulary with a vague but composed interest; he might have been studying the logistics of a homicide operation from the detached but informed standpoint of the military historian he was.

Appleby wondered, somewhat inconsequently, whether Ledward had ever seen anything of this sort before. Had gentlemen with swords at their sides, or ornate in satin, or buckskin-breeched from hunting, ever fallen in their cups to some lethal quarrel amid all this tomb-like splendour and massive decorum? A film director could mount a splendid armed brawl as eddying round these ranked columns. The poised and planted feet would ring on marble, and the smooth alabaster be grooved and gashed by the flailing blades. At the moment, however, the only camera on the scene had just been carried into the drawing-room by an officer in plain clothes; he would take numerous photographs of the corpse; on some future day, perhaps, a judge would examine these, and decide that the more distressing of them need not be placed in the hands of the jury.

'I hear they have broken up the octagon room,' Professor Snodgrass said, a little unexpectedly. 'It has never seemed to me other than in poor taste. But to take a hammer to it has been exceedingly high-handed, to my mind.'

'It wasn't exactly a matter of a hammer.' The chronic mild battiness of Beddoes Snodgrass, Appleby reflected, might well cause Detective Inspector Stride to despair of him as a reliable witness. But of course the old gentleman was perfectly capable of responding to reason with reason – or intermittently so, at least. 'And I'm afraid I was partly responsible myself. I was trying to catch somebody, you know. One of those South Americans.'

This piece of shock tactics was not without its effect. The Professor gave Appleby a glance the sharpness of which didn't wholly cohere with his general air of being perched at some remove above the general level of events.

'South Americans, my dear Sir Edward?'

'John.'

'Ah, yes – Sir John. It takes time to place a new neighbour. You think that is the explanation of my poor nephew's being shot? It hadn't occurred to me. But nothing is more likely. A mission of vengeance on the part of Gozman Spinto's crowd. Adrian smashed Gozman Spinto, you know. It was a great step towards constitutional government.'

'I understand it was your ancester the Liberator who smashed Gozman Spinto. Decapitated him, in fact. And that it wasn't a great step to anything except the Liberator's making a packet.'

'Really? Well, the details are unimportant, are they not. Emissaries of one scoundrelly Azuera *Junta* or another. Do you think they may still be lurking in Ledward? If so, I am inclined to suggest that the military be called to the asssitance of the police. The villains may be in possession of automatic weapons. They are said to be coming increasingly into use.'

'I hardly think, Professor, that soldiers are required.'

'Well, mention it to me, if you change your mind. There is no doubt a militia regiment quite near at hand. The Lord Lieutenant of the County would know. He is an old friend of mine, and I could call upon him at any time.'

'Thank you. I'll bear it in mind. I wonder whether you can tell me . . .'

'I have asked Leonidas to serve coffee. The hour appears to be somewhat advanced. But it didn't seem to me that we had quite got to the stage of early morning tea. Besides, that is best partaken of in bed.'

'Certainly it is. But what I want to ask you about is connected with South America, and Adrian's long sojourns there. Do you think his wife came back to England with him on this occasion?'

'Adrian's *wife*? I don't know what you're talking about.'

'But didn't you tell me that he had a wife? And a little boy?'

'Nothing of the kind.' Professor Snodgrass had suddenly produced what Appleby characterized to himself as a glare of cold sanity. 'You must have taken leave of your senses.'

'Not quite that, I hope. But no doubt I misunderstood you, or am confusing your family with another family having connections out there.' Appleby offered this absurdity without a blush. It was only fair, after all, to send an occasional imbecile vagueness back over the net, so to speak, and into the Professor's court. 'So there's no direct heir to Ledward? How very sad! That such a splendid place should in a fashion be going begging.' Appleby shook his head in a sombre fashion – and then seemed to cheer up, as if another thought had struck him. 'But, of course, Adrian *may* have married, and without troubling to let you know about it. Any time in these past ten years, or thereabout. Indeed, nothing is more probable. He was just the age at which his type often decides to settle down. Adventure and women and so forth behind him, and a stable and domestic life in front. Such marriages are often singularly happy and successful. With your experience of the world, Professor, you must have noticed that. And it's particularly true in cases in which there's more than a mere competence in the way of family fortune. Yes, Adrian, come to think of it, had almost certainly married. And he'd come back to fix up his future manner of life here. He'd be looking forward to the boy's growing up in the old home. The first pony. The first gun. Off to Eton for his first half. All that. It can still happen, of course, so far as the little chap is concerned. I wonder whether he takes after both the Snodgrasses and the Beddoeses.'

Appleby paused with some satisfaction on this rapidly constructed fantasy. *We are not now that strength which in old days moved earth and heaven*, he was telling himself. *Still we can give a kick or two now and then*. And thus vaingloriously congratulating himself, he had another rapid go.

'I expect,' he said, 'you know Charles Pumpernickle? He's our ambassador in Patagonia at the moment. And of course it was he who told me, not you. Stupid of me to make that muddle. Told me, I mean, about Adrian Snodgrass's marriage. And about the boy. A dear little fellow, he says.'

It would not have been possible to maintain that Professor Beddoes Snodgrass displayed any marked gratification at thus being suddenly dowered with a great-nephew – even one vouched for as a dear little fellow. On the other hand (and Appleby was watching him closely) he gave no sign of mortification or rage. Perhaps he was sufficiently in possession of his wits to know very well that he had been listening to an outrageous fabrication. Or perhaps his regard and affection had been wholly for Adrian as an individual, so that, with Adrian

dead, he wasn't much affected by Appleby's story, even if he
believed it. Or perhaps, yet again, his mental life was in fact
so discontinuous that Stride was justified in feeling that nothing was to be done with him. Appleby, however, had one last
shot.

'I am sure,' he said (not very decently, but policemen cannot always be over-nice), 'that this will be a great consolation
to you. The fact, I mean, that Adrian has left a son. But will it
come as a disappointment to somebody else?'

'Somebody else?'

'There must be somebody who would be due to inherit
Ledward now, if Adrian had *not* in fact married and produced
an heir. Who is he?'

'He?'

'You mean it's a woman?'

'Leonidas – I wonder what can have become of him.' Whether through guile or not, Professor Snodgrass had gone completely vague again. 'Why hasn't he brought that coffee? But
– dear me! – now I remember. I have dismissed him.'

'Dismissed Leonidas? Given him notice?'

'Or did he dismiss me?' The Professor paused, and appeared to see no light on this problem. 'He certainly remarked
that these were not respectable goings-on. It was hard to con-
trovert him. Unfortunately, what he had to say was couched in
a tone of some insolence. So he has departed. That's why
there's no coffee. I do, my dear fellow, apologize about it.'

'Never mind about the coffee. You say your butler has *departed*?'

'Certainly. Returned in his car to the Old Dower House,
packed his bags – and by this time will have cleared out for
good. You may make your mind entirely easy, Appleby. You
won't see that rather objectionable man again. He has been a
disappointment to me, I'm bound to say. One has a right to
expect more of a person with a name like that. Weren't we having a chat, by the way, about Thermopylae? We must resume
it, one day.'

'Yes, indeed.' Appleby felt a strong prompting to seize Beddoes Snodgrass and shake him vigorously. 'May I ask whether
the police know about Leonidas's departure?'

'I doubt whether he mentioned it to them, my dear Appleby. Nor have I. After all, it can't really concern them. And they appear to have such a lot on their hands as it is, poor fellows. Do you know' – and Professor Snodgrass suddenly brightened – 'I think I'll go and make that coffee myself?'

Part Three First Light

Chapter Fourteen

This was a house – Appleby told himself as he watched the Professor totter away on his stick – in which reliable informaton remained in uncommonly short supply. On the other hand the place was willing to do one any amount of solitude, and it was in solitude that such scant information as he had managed to acquire might best be sifted and reflected upon. No doubt if he returned to the society of Inspector Stride he might pick up a little more hard fact than he was yet possessed of, and certain areas of the mystery might emerge from the soft focus in which they were at present obstinately clothed for him. But for half an hour or so they could wait. He would simply lose himself in Ledward and brood.

There was one direction in which he had not yet gone. This was along the fourth of the quadrant corridors and into whatever it conducted to. Presumably this would be a wing of the same general dimensions as the other three. One might make a bet with oneself as to what it housed. For instance, it might be devoted to a museum of South American antiquities, and even contain pictures and records of value in trying to get a notion of the character of the Snodgrasses' involvement in the continent. Or it might be divided in two, like the wing shared by the hothouse and the chapel, and offer the alternative diversions of a billiard-room and a swimming-bath. Appleby decided to take his ruminative stroll in that direction.

Had he really got anything out of Professor Snodgrass on the strength of the nonsense he had talked to him? He certainly hadn't elicited anything dramatic. Neither a howl of rage nor an expression of unbounded joy had greeted his confident assertion that Adrian had left an infant heir behind him. Again, the Professor had not been drawn into any communication as to whom *he* understood or supposed that Ledward would now pass. His avoidance of this had something wary or nervous about it. And there was another odd thing: he had shown no impulse to be communicative about his own glimpse of the marauders.

After all, at least one of the men *had* been a sinister-looking foreigner. Appleby had described him to Stride accurately enough. And when he had spoken of them to the Professor as 'those South Americans' the old gentleman had accepted this and elaborated upon it within a matter of seconds. But this had taken the form of a piece of extravagant chronological confusion. And it had *not* prompted him to add, in corroboration of the general idea of some exotic vendetta, that his own glimpse had undoubtedly been of Latin-American persons. Yet the effect of that glimpse had, for a time, been shattering – or, if not shattering, bewildering. And Snodgrass had now shut down on it.

One must concede the possibility, Appleby reflected, of two distinct crimes. It was untidy; it wouldn't please Dr Absolon in his character as a connoisseur of detective fiction; but one had to come back to it, all the same. Two synchronous crimes – but not grossly coincidental, since each had keyed to the same brief span of time for logical reasons. The intruders whom he himself had glimpsed (who might, or might not, have been those whom the Professor and Mrs Anglebury had severally glimpsed) were indeed exotic. They had pursued Adrian Snodgrass, it might be, across the South Atlantic Ocean. But their purpose, conceivably, had not been vendetta or vengeance, but something quite different. And there were a number of possibilities here, although the most obvious of them connected itself with the rifled safe. These foreigners (former associates of Adrian's, or whatever they may have been) knew enough about the safe to hunt for it. *And they had wanted to get to it first*. They had wanted to abstract or destroy vital papers, say, before Adrian himself recovered and in some way exploited them. And it looked as if they had succeeded, more or less.

The other intruders had been English – since it had been 'lower-class urban voices' that Dr Absolon had heard. These people had come on this particular night simply because it was the night in the year upon which Ledward and its treasures were uniquely vulnerable. They, too, had been successful, since they had departed with the Claude and much else. And everything pointed to them as the killers of Adrian Snodgrass. That sort of killing is the product of a loss of nerve. As cool and efficient criminals they seemed inferior to the other lot.

And so much, Appleby thought, by way of a preliminary guess or two. It was a picture of the affair which at least organized some of the main chunks of evidence into the semblance of a coherent pattern. Still, as a nearly completed jigsaw in which all the remaining pieces showed promise of using themselves up it wasn't possible to think very highly of it.

Confronting this gloomy conclusion, Appleby came to a halt and looked about him. This quadrant corridor wasn't identical with the others. It was, so to speak, a de luxe model, with an impressive additional feature thrown in. On its outer curve, which was on his left as he walked, it opened out into a semi-circular apse-like recess which looked large enough to accommodate a small orchestra. What it did accommodate was an indifferent marble reproduction of the Laocoön Group. The unfortunate father and his sons, writhing in the coils of Athena's avenging serpents, had been combined with a placid little fountain which (like everything else at Ledward that night) had been paraded for the returning heir. There was a marble bench in front of the exhibition, as if to invite the passer-by to a leisured gloat before this revolting masterpiece of the Pergamene school. Appleby sat down and regarded it glumly. One had to admit that here was a spectacle of violence which *had* been tidied up. Polydorus, Athenodorus, and Agesander (if those were really the sculptors' names) had reduced those straining bodies and contorted limbs to a tolerably lucid spectacle artistically regarded. They hadn't, so to speak, left anything out of their particular jigsaw. Appleby got up and moved on. He must try to emulate just that.

He continued down the corridor. It happened to be one of those patches of Ledward that was poorly lit, and when Appleby opened a door at its end and stepped into brilliant

115

illumination he was for some moments at a loss to interpret what confronted him. He seemed to be in a small structure like a wooden horse-box, and looking out through an unglazed aperture at a lofty and enormous hall which might conceivably be a riding-school. Along the whole of one wall there was a low wooden structure, like a projecting corridor, with netted openings here and there, and a sloping wooden roof. High overhead there were windows and a skylight, but the present shadowless lighting came from a very modern-looking electrical installation just below the rafters. By way of making a little more of this, Appleby took a couple of steps forward. As he did so there was the sound of something like a sharp report from somewhere in front of him, instantly followed by an ugly crack against the woodwork behind. He was just reflecting that the night's show-down had really begun (and had in fact dropped swiftly to the floor) when a triumphant voice sounded from somewhere at the other end of the hall.

'Got the dedans!'

'And you nearly got me.' Appleby had risen rather sheepishly to his feet. 'And you're serving from the hazard side. Come over here, and see if you can get the grille.'

'I'm terribly sorry. I'd no idea anybody would come along here.' David Anglebury had jumped over the sagging net which gives its delusively slapdash suggestion to a real-tennis court, still carrying a couple of balls and the oddly lopsided racquet with which the ancient game is played. 'I was just mucking around,' he said. 'I didn't feel like going to sleep in this damned house. And, of course, I can't leave until my mother can.'

'Dr Plumridge has settled her down for a bit?'

'Yes – but the police want to ask her all sorts of things. Only as part of the drill, I think.'

'I'm not sure that I quite know what you mean by that, Mr Anglebury.'

'Well, they know about her, you see.'

'In just what way? Has she a habit of going round confessing to other people's crimes? Forgive me if that sounds rather crude. It's a species of morbid behaviour, as a matter of fact, known to every experienced police officer. The trouble is, you'll understand, that one never can tell.'

'I suppose so.' Without warning, the young man swung round, and sent first one, and then the other small solid ball he was holding viciously across the net. 'I don't really play this ruddy game. You have to be rather grand for it. Lord's, or Queen's Club.'

'Or be the owner of Ledward Park.'

'Well, yes. That's obvious. And you can see the court's in excellent order, like everything else here. Waiting for Adrian Snodgrass – and now this happens! It's rather a rotten show, really.'

'Certainly it is. But the question is, how rotten? Don't you think?'

'I don't understand that at all, sir.'

'Perhaps I'm just being crude once more. But put it this way. If Adrian was killed by a reckless thief he'd cornered, that was less rotten. If he was killed by a close relation, that was more rotten. Or am I taking an old-fashioned view?'

'You're suggesting the possibility of something monstrous.' David Anglebury looked straight at Appleby. 'I suppose it has been your trade.'

'I suppose it has. Well, let's go and discuss this in company of something else that's monstrous, and that will set the tone. I mean the Laocoön in the corridor. One can at least sit down there.'

'Very well, sir.' With no sign of reluctance, the young man let his racquet drop to the floor. 'But I'm afraid I'll only be saying again what I've already said to your subordinate.'

'Inspector Stride isn't my subordinate. He's an independent concern – and, of course, the official one, for that matter. As for saying the same thing over again, it mayn't work out that way. Our talk may take a different turn.'

'I'm not going to contradict myself, if that's what you mean.' David Anglebury had flushed suddenly. 'I'm hiding nothing at all. Not even about my mother.'

'Thank you. Now, come along.'

The Laocoön Group was as it had been. Neither the Trojan

117

prince and his sons nor the serpents had made any progress. There was something unnatural about their immobility which made a returning spectator uneasy. The critic Lessing, Appleby supposed, had been getting at something like this in his celebrated book that took its title from the work.

'Nemesis of a Detective,' David Anglebury said.

'I beg your pardon?'

'The ugly thing might be called that. Laocoön did a little too much deduction about the Trojan Horse – managed to see through it, you might say. And this is what came to him as a result. And to his kids too. You might regard it as a kind of cautionary tale, sir.'

'So I might. Or so might any young man who found himself caught up in the toils of something he hadn't any very clear view of the origin of.' Appleby paused, not very pleased with this retort. Young Anglebury wasn't the completely simple-minded boy he'd taken him to be. There had been a certain wit in the notion of Laocoön as an injudicious meddler in mysteries. But it still was quite uncertain how much he knew about himself. And to go fishing now for what he might have discovered or been told about his parentage was not, to Appleby's mind, an agreeable occupation. He almost regretted his proposal to continue this talk. But he was in for it now. So was the boy.

'Mr Anglebury, you didn't like my speaking about the possibility of this being a family crime. But many murders are. As a matter of fact, most people (like myself) who have had to do with it are inclined to see murder as a very special sort of thing. In a way, it's often hardly like a crime at all – even although, paradoxically, it comes right at the top of the list of crimes. A murderer is rather like a duke: a nobleman, but yet quite different from other sorts of noblemen.' Appleby kept an eye on David Anglebury as he rapidly advanced this thesis, and was aware that it had been accorded genuine attention. He was confirmed in his view that the young man was intelligent. 'But I was saying that a substantial proportion of murders are inside-the-family affairs. A sexual motive is distinguishable in many of them – as it is in so many imaginative works involving killings, from Greek tragedy down to the present day. But an even larger number turn on property or inheritance. The largest single group is concened with property in the humblest way. What the old woman is believed to keep under her bed, or to have in the post-office savings bank. That sort of thing.'

'How very dismal and horrible.'

'It doesn't have the glamour of Clytemnestra, I agree.'

'Even Lady Macbeth doesn't have that. She was only after what King Duncan had in the till – or the wardrobe.'

'I suppose that's true.' Appleby's mental note was now to the effect that Anglebury was really clever. 'But all this is beating about the bush. There is every appearance of Adrian Snodgrass's having been killed by thieves whom he had surprised at their work. And it may well turn out that way. But other possibilities have to be considered, as you very well know. It looks as if, yesterday, there weren't too many people around who so much as certainly knew whether the man was still alive or not. Then he turns up; *is* alive; and gets killed. I ought to add at once that the crime may have had a political motive. Because, as it happens . . .'

'I must say I find it hard to believe that one.' Rather to Appleby's surprise, Anglebury had broken in crisply with this. 'I understand the general idea. Adrian Snodgrass had made enemies in Azuera, and some of them followed him home here and killed him. Have you read much about recent Latin-American history, sir?'

'I can't say that I have. It's an interest of your own?'

'Well, yes. I've read quite a number of books about it from time to time.'

'I find that most interesting, Mr Anglebury.'

'Do you?' Appleby received one of the young man's straight looks. 'What I was going to say is this. Politics can be pretty tough in a good many countries over there. But I don't think the contestants pursue each other from continent to continent with revolvers. That's the principle of the vendetta, isn't it? I don't think it has much established itself in those places. Perhaps I'm speaking on much too little real information – and, of course, I have no first-hand knowledge of South Americans and their ways whatever. But I just have a feel of

119

this idea as wrong. As astray, I mean. I find myself not believing in it.'

'I'm not sure I don't agree with you. But, you know, the murder may have been unpremeditated. Indeed, it has very much the appearance of that. Former associates of the dead man may have come here to confer with him – or say to bargain with him – and then something may have gone wrong, so that some fatal fracas followed. Or the meeting may have been interrupted by something having nothing to do with it.'

'By thieves operating on their own, for instance. Or by relations lured on by the thought of what Adrian Snodgrass had in the post-office savings bank. Or hidden under his bed – but that, it seems, turned out just to be my mother.'

'We needn't take that up just at the moment.' Appleby hardly knew what to make of the remark just offered to him. It was a heartless joke, and not engaging. But perhaps it was some sort of desperation that had prompted it. 'What I'm really in search of – and being rather obstinately denied – is authentic family history.'

'Snodgrass family history, I suppose you mean. But I don't see how you can imagine I'm going to help you to it.'

'Perhaps your mother can help. Hasn't she been a family friend for a long time?'

'You know very well there's no sense in that, and that my mother's mind is very badly deranged. She might say anything under the sun. But her doctors would have to tell you that you couldn't believe a word of it.'

'That may be an exaggeration, I think. What your mother had to say might be informative, if only in a fragmentary fashion.'

'I don't want her bothered, sir!' This came from the young man like a cry. 'It might have the most ghastly effect on her.'

'I understand your feeling, Mr Anglebury. Unfortunately your mother turned up here tonight in very odd circumstances – and yourself after her, for that matter. The police have an inescapable duty at least to seek to question her. I really don't see how they can be headed off – unless the necessary information can be obtained elsewhere. I think myself that the mystery – and it *is* a mystery, goodness knows – may be connected with events long before your time. Or *just* before your time.' Appleby paused. 'But I don't think I ought to go on with this. I have nothing to do with the local police; I'm at Ledward by sheer accident; and it's open to you to conclude that I'm actuated by nothing except vulgar and morbid curiosity.'

There was a moment's silence.

'I think I'd like to tell you what I can,' David Anglebury said.

Chapter Fifteen

Laocoön was doing quite well; he had one of the serpents firmly by the neck. But his sons, although well-grown lads, were not being much help; they seemed chiefly concerned to achieve a despairing gesture. The little fountain dribbled and prattled inconsequently at their feet. Appleby found the effect irritating, and was rather inclined to lead David Anglebury elsewhere. But the tennis-court had been comfortless, and to retreat in the other direction would be to return to the vicinity of Stride and his assistants. It would be best to stay put, and listen to the young man while – so to speak – the listening was good.

'I sometimes think that my mother must have brought herself up on bad Victorian novels.' Anglebury seemed unconscious that this was an odd introduction to what he might have to say. 'Did you ever read Hardy's *Tess of the d'Urbervilles*?'

'Yes, of course.' Appleby was surprised. 'But that's not a bad Victorian novel. It's a very good one.'

'I know it is. But, you see, I've been reading English at Cambridge, and I found out something odd about it.'

'About Cambridge?'

'About Thomas Hardy's novel. The way one reads it now, the heroine just gets seduced by the villain, Alec d'Urberville. He takes her home from a rustics' dance one night, and his ardour is a bit too much for her, and he simply manages to have her in a wood. He's a nasty chap, but the thing is natural enough in itself.'

'I suppose that is so.' Appleby saw no reason to hurry young Anglebury. This preamble was a kind of staving off of embarrassing matter to come.

'But what I discovered was this. When Hardy wanted to start by printing the novel as a serial in a magazine, he wasn't allowed to arrange Tess's seduction like that, because it wouldn't have been respectable, or at all a proper start for a heroine's career. So he had to take out the bit in the wood – it's called a chase, actually – and put in something extremely silly about Tess's having been hoodwinked by a bogus marriage-ceremony. And apparently there were lots of bad novels full of rubbish of that kind, and Hardy was just taking over a standard melodramatic device.'

'I see.' Appleby paused. 'And you think,' he said gently, 'that your mother had been a reader of them? They'd have been rather out of date, you know, even when she was a girl.'

'I expect I'm talking rot, really.' Anglebury, who was sitting stiffly upright on his bench, had flushed swiftly; and the effect of this was curiously enhanced by the bleakly white marble of the Laocoön Group and their niche. 'But well, sir, you understand what I'm saying, more or less.'

'What you know came to you from your mother?'

'Yes – and when most of her mind was quite sensible. When it was only in bits and pieces that she had taken to imagining things. She was imagining that she had been tricked into going through a false marriage ceremony. I suppose it's conceivable that a servant-girl might be deceived in that way. But it couldn't happen to a lady. To an educated woman, I mean.'

'It does seem improbable.'

'But the ... the *thing* happened, all right. The seduction or whatever it's to be called. And I'm afraid I've got rather a staggerer for you now, sir. It was Adrian Snodgrass. I'm his illegitimate son.'

'I see.' Although without feigning surprise, Appleby gave no indication that this was not altogether a novel idea to him. 'Would you say that many people know?'

'Oh, yes – I think so. At least some must. I'm said to be rather like him, as a matter of fact.'

Appleby had got up abruptly and moved over to the fountain. He might have been searching for a tap which should enable him to turn the confounded thing off. He had, in fact, found young David's last remark curiously touching. A boy has to take some sort of pride in his parentage, and here had been an oblique way of expressing it. There had been a staunchness, a kind of standing up to be counted, in it, as well. And now the lad's father had met a violent death and his mother had been crazily claiming to have inflicted it. Appleby found himself liking the Ledward affair less and less. But it would at least be a shade less uncomfortable as past history, and that was what he had to make it. He had something like three hours, he reckoned, until that notional breakfast-time.

'So the story is this,' he said. 'Your father got your mother with child, and then deserted her. And you are the child. You may well regard it as unforgivable. There have been sons who have grown up to exact vengeance in such circumstances.'

'I suppose so.' For a moment Anglebury's taut body sagged, so that he suddenly looked very tired. 'But if I'd killed my father, I think I'd have told you by now.'

'That is the probability, I agree.' Appleby was unemotional. 'But not, of course, a certainty. I suppose, by the way, that what your father did – or what you believe him to have done – does horrify you?'

'Yes – but not as much as somebody having killed him does. I try to be objective. As a matter of fact, I once got so desperate that I had a talk with the family doctor about it . . .'

'You mean Dr Plumridge?'

'Yes. We've known him for a long time.'

'I see. Go on.'

'He helped me to see that I must try to hold the balance even. My mother may have been very unstable from the first, and that may be why my father funked honourable marriage.'

'Yes. But she wasn't too unstable to get married to someone else quickly enough to avoid open scandal. Or have I got it wrong?'

'You've got it quite right. Charles Anglebury was some sort of lawyer. He had fallen deeply in love with my mother some years before. Or so my mother has told me at times when she was sane enough.'

'And he knew.'

'Oh, yes – I'm sure he did. The whole thing. He was some sort of minor saint, I think.'

'You liked him, and as a boy took it for granted that he was your father?'

'I remember nothing about him. I was very small when he died.'

'And were you very small when your mother began confiding this unhappy story to you?'

'It depends what you mean by small. I suppose I was about eight.'

This information again brought Appleby to something of a halt. But he was committed now to extracting from the boy everything he was willing to tell.

'About that faked marriage service,' he said. 'It turns up, as a matter of fact, in plenty of plays and romances long before the Victorian age. Do you think your mother told this particular part of her story to others as well as yourself?'

'I know she did.' David Anglebury shrugged his shoulders awkwardly, so that one could see he wasn't given to such gestures. 'It was one of the first things to show the doctors and people she was a little mad. You don't think they should have believed her, do you?'

'I am quite sure they oughtn't to have disbelieved her without investigation. Did she tell the story in any circumstantial detail, so that some sort of check-up could have been made?'

'I don't think so. Certainly not to me.'

'Did she come here, and did you follow her here, a year ago tonight?'

'Yes – but nobody else knew. She had just wandered into the house, when I arrived and got her away. I didn't tell Dr Plumridge or anybody. I knew perfectly well, you see, that it was all entirely harmless. Even although she talked rather as she talked this time. The wronged woman business. I've got in the way of not creating about all this. What would be the good? It doesn't seem as if they can do anything. And it would be a bit heart-breaking, really, if I didn't manage to take it more or less in my stride. It's lucky we have money – not a great deal, but enough. We have a very capable woman at home. She was a nurse.'

'That's something. But the future must take some planning for. I suppose you haven't come down from Cambridge yet?

'Oh, no. I go back for my second year next week.' The young man hesitated. 'If this affair doesn't go on being too awkward, that is.'

'It won't.'

'You are sure of that, sir?' Anglebury sounded surprised and relieved.

'Yes. A case of this sort – one has to call it a case – always gets itself cleared up quickly.' Appleby paused on this; he was now facing the seated boy squarely. 'Where there is abundance of mystery and confusion in every direction, the truth seldom remains hidden for long. It's a matter of having plenty of angles to go at it from. Only the utterly simple crimes – the simplex crimes, you might say – have the trick of remaining baffling.'

'Well, that's rather good news.' Anglebury, although puzzled, appeared genuinely cheered up. 'Is there anything else I can possibly be useful about, sir?'

'There are several matters I'd like more information on, as a matter of fact. This house, for example. You give me the impression of knowing it pretty well. Do you come here quite a lot?'

'Not really that.' A slight return of wariness was observable in Anglebury's manner.

'You know your way to that tennis court, for instance, and find it quite natural to knock a ball about there. But Ledward must surely be shut up for most of the time – although of course there has been this bizarre yearly occasion.'

'Professor Snodgrass works in the house fairly regularly. And his people come and go. Leonidas, for example. It's with him I've played tennis, as a matter of fact. He taught me.'

'The Professor's butler – or late butler – taught you to play real tennis! Didn't you find his ability to do that a bit odd?'

'Well, no. One mustn't be snobbish.'

'My dear young man, that's about the first inconsequent thing you've said.'

'I'm sorry. Getting tired, I suppose. I'm not used to what they call interrogation. And you have the technique, all right, in a mild way. I notice how you manoeuvre me into facing the light, for one thing.'

For a moment Appleby made no reply to this – which was in fact a perfectly valid observation. He hadn't, he told himself, really decided about David Anglebury. The boy seemed more honestly communicative by a long way than anybody else he had encountered at Ledward so far. But his very facility seemed worth thnking about. So did the impulse he occasionally betrayed to square up as for combat.

'I suppose Leonidas may have been in service somewhere where the game is played.' Appleby appeared to dismiss the matter. 'Yes, that would be it.'

'I've thought of something else, as a matter of fact.' Anglebury hesitated. 'I don't know quite how to put it. You might call me snobbish again.'

'But I didn't call you snobbish! It was you yourself who used the word.'

'So it was.' Anglebury made what was only his second gesture during this interview: a passing of a hand across his eyes. 'I think Leonidas may be what they used to call a fallen gentleman.'

'I hadn't thought of that one.' Appleby regarded the young man soberly. 'But tell me a little more about your coming to Ledward from time to time. It must have been more or less by way of invitation from Professor Snodgrass?'

'Yes, of course. He's always been very decent. Mildly friendly, you know.'

'I can see him being that. I suppose, by the way, he knows – well, your family history?'

'My parentage, you mean?' There had been an upward tilt to Anglebury's chin as he asked this. 'I imagine so. I don't really know. He's never said anything about it. Of course he's rather deep, wouldn't you say?'

'Deep?' Simple-minded surprise was what Appleby appeared to register. 'He strikes me as rather rambling and senile. But perhaps you're right.'

'Perhaps he could be both.' Anglebury had glanced with a swift suspicion at Appleby. He might be tired, Appleby thought. But he remained unobtrusively a very sharp young man indeed.

'May I ask you one further question, Mr Anglebury?'

'Yes, of course. But I'm not terribly fond, by the way, of being called Mr Anglebury. I'd rather you called me David – even if you still nurse the darkest thoughts about me.'

'David, then. And as for the darkest thoughts, it's my business to nurse these about pretty well everybody, right up to the moment I sign off.'

'Which is going to be quite soon?'

'Quite soon.'

'I begin to believe you,' David Anglebury said.

Appleby's reply to this had been to nod absently, and to take a short turn down the corridor and back.

'I really can't stand any more of Laocoön,' he said. 'Why can't the creatures finish their job, kids and all? Why look at this horrid frozen thing when you can read Virgil?'

'Why, indeed, sir? You're a very sophisticated policeman.'

'And you, young man, are quite some way from being the best type of English public-school boy – manly but thick. However, that's by the way. My final question is about your father. As far as I can gather, he hasn't been seen in these parts for eight or ten years. Not since you were quite a small boy.'

'Not all that small.'

'Precisely. So did you meet him? Have you any impression of him?'

'Yes.'

'Was this after your mother had told you her story?'

'Yes.'

'So you were aware that you were meeting your father – who nevertheless was somehow not your father? It was like that?'

'Just like that. You'll think I'm cracked about English novels. But Joseph Conrad . . .'

'I know, David. In *Under Western Eyes* the obscure student, Razumov, is introduced into the presence of Prince K—, who is in fact his father. But no reference to this illegitimate paternity is made. You're saying it was like that?'

'Yes, except that Razumov wasn't a child.'

'And your father would have known who you were?'

'Of course.'

'I know it's a very distant thing to be talking about, or trying to recover. But can you give me any impression of how he – well, carried it off?'

'Beautifully.'

There was a silence. Perhaps this single word was ambiguous, Appleby thought. It might be used with some derogatory or ironic implication. Yet it hadn't sounded like that. And this suddenly seemed to Appleby a circumstance stranger than anything that had turned up upon him on this not unremarkable night.

'Beautifully?' he repeated.

'Just that, sir. And it had nothing to do with carrying the thing off – although I suppose he must have been conscious that there *was* something very much in need of carrying off. There I stood – a gentleman's son, if we may be snobbish again, and going by the name of Anglebury. And there *he* was. Well, he was just very nice. If I'd been grown-up, I'd have phrased it that he showed extraordinary delicacy. He didn't show affection, because that wouldn't have been delicate.'

'But the affection was potentially there?'

'Yes.'

'David, you say you were quite small – and it's chronologically self-evident that you were. These were remarkable things for a small boy to feel. May you not be projecting back upon the actual occasion feelings that you came to imagine about it long afterwards?'

'No.'

This second monosyllable had for a moment the effect of silencing Appleby. He glanced from David to the Laocoön Group and back again.

'Stop sitting there as if you were stuffed,' he found himself exclaiming oddly. 'Get on your feet, and walk with me up this damned hypertrophied corridor.' He waited until the boy did as he was told. 'You left that encounter wishing very much that this man who was your father wasn't your father with some mysterious difference?'

'Just that.' David Anglebury, now pacing beside Appleby, turned his head and glanced at him stonily. 'And I think he may have had a similar feeling. But nothing more happened – not ever again. Incidentally, sir, you spoke of chronology. But you have only an approximate notion of it. I can give it to you exactly. I last saw my father – alive, that is, and not rather unmistakably dead – nine years, three months, and a week from today.'

In a long silence the two men – or the man and the boy – reached the end of the corridor: the damned hypertrophied corridor in this damned hypertrophied house. In front of them, and in turn giving upon the enormous pillared hall, was a nondescript room which Appleby had marked as probably once an office used in connection with the business of the estate. It looked as if they must shortly present themselves once more to Inspector Stride and his men.

'I implied that I was asking my last question,' Appleby said. 'But I have another one, after all. If things had happened differently, you would be inheriting Ledward tonight. As it is, *somebody* is inheriting it. The property is passing to somebody, man or woman, whom I'll call X. And the identity of X – which must be the simplest matter in the world – is precisely what nobody has yet condescended to reveal to me. David, can you tell me who X is?'

'I can tell you.'

The door before them had opened, and the figure of a man stood framed in it.

'I am X,' the man said.

Chapter Sixteen

The stranger – who had thus appeared to Appleby's notably astonished gaze pat like the catastrophe of the old comedy – was best to be described as well-groomed. Like the lord who annoyed young Hotspur in the aftermath of battle, he was neat and trimly dressed; and if not positively perfumed like a milliner, he did faintly exude a hint of expensive soaps and lotions as in some glossy advertisement for masculine *chic*. Appleby found all this untimely – perhaps for no better reason than that he himself had been up throughout the night, and was for various reasons (including a great deal of charging around and one quite stiff fight) feeling in a somewhat Hotspur-like disarray.

'My name is Basil Snodgrass,' the stranger said to Appleby. 'And if you are the stray London detective I've just been told about, I've no doubt you have heard of me.'

'I have done nothing of the kind.' Appleby (although the description wasn't wholly unjust) had taken no pleasure in hearing himself described as a stray London detective. 'If I had, I should not have been asking Mr Anglebury for information the nature of which you seem to have overheard while listening on the other side of that door.'

'Well, it's my own door, after all.' Basil Snodgrass appeared amused. 'As for what you were asking this young man, I took that to have been just some police dodge or other. But has Beddoes really not mentioned me? I find that very odd. At least it must have been he who told his butler to ring me up with this shocking news.'

'Leonidas rang you up?'

'Leonidas? That may have been his name, although it sounds a deuced odd one. Not that I couldn't cap it. I once had a handyman called Pneumaticos.' Basil Snodgrass offered this useless information with an air of wishing to modify a certain acerbity which had so far marked his tone. 'It wouldn't be easy to beat that, eh? But, as I was saying, this fellow got me out of bed in the small hours, and told me about Adrian's death. He wasn't at all civil about it. He seemed to feel that butlers in decent houses are not required to make such communications.'

'As a matter of fact, Leonidas is understood to have left Professor Snodgrass's employment on much that score.'

'A good riddance, no doubt. And we could do with a rather more general exodus from Ledward, if you ask me. Clumping coppers all over the place.'

'I am afraid, Mr Snodgrass, that as things stand at the moment there would be little point in attempting to order the police off the premises. But as soon as the obscurity surrounding the late Mr Snodgrass's death is cleared up – and I expect it to be quite soon – they will certainly depart gladly enough. Certainly I shall.'

'My dear sir, I have no wish to be inhospitable.' Basil Snodgrass was again conciliatory. 'Not even to this young man, who is totally unknown to me.'

'My name is David Anglebury.' David was looking angry. 'And this is Sir John Appleby, and I think it may be rather lucky that he has turned up.'

'Anglebury? Ah. yes. Well, we are now known to each other, all three.'

'Am I correct,' Appleby asked, 'in supposing you to be a brother of Adrian Snodgrass?'

'A half-brother. There are now no surviving children or descendants of our father's first marriage, and I am the only child of his second. So there is nothing at all complicated about me.' Basil Snodgrass suddenly produced what could not in fairness have been called other than a charming smile; some mechanism of social appraisal, it was to be presumed, had prompted him to modify his attitude to Appleby. 'And I'm sorry to have announced myself as I did. Considering the situation in this house, it was in rather indifferent taste, no doubt. I'm afraid I have something of a theatrical streak about me. Perhaps I oughtn't even to have hurried over, really. But I thought I might give poor old Beddoes a bit of support. Not that we've ever been in the least intimate. There's something there, indeed, that may puzzle you: my giving the effect of having so much dropped out of the blue.'

'Or the black,' Appleby said. 'It's still quite some time till dawn.'

'Quite so. I live, I ought to say, about fifty miles off – but my contacts with the Ledward Snodgrasses have been tenuous, all the same. No malice; it has just happened like that. Ages ago, my father made a totally new life for himself with his new marriage, and the families have continued that way.'

'Its not uncommon, where there have been two marriages.'

'Quite so. And, of course, I've been abroad a great deal. I'm just back from Brazil, as a matter of fact.'

'Brazil? Then I take it you are another of the Snodgrasses with South American connections?'

'Oh, yes. It's a family thing, you might say. Even old Beddoes, who has nothing either political or commercial about him. He has published text-books about some of the beastly wars over there.'

'I'm not sure how much you will have learnt from the police, Mr Snodgrass. Did they tell you that we appear to have had South American callers at Ledward tonight?'

'Yes, they did – and I'm bound to say I think it a thoroughly unlikely story. This business of a Poussin . . .'

'A Claude.'

'Ah, yes. It has never much occurred to me to find out about the Ledward treasures. There has been no particular reason, after all, to suppose that I would outlive Adrian. But, as I say, this picture-stealing affair just doesn't square with notions of political assassination, or whatever it's supposed to have been. You might be caught stealing a picture, and shoot the man who jumped at you. But you wouldn't kill a man because you disliked his politics, or because he knew inconveniently much about yours, and then walk off with his Claude as a kind of luck-penny.'

'That is true. It seems almost necessary to believe that your half-brother's return to Ledward precipitated several operations not very intimately connected with one another.'

'Several?'

'Well, say a couple that embodied some criminal intention' – Appleby glanced at David Anglebury – 'and one other that

132

might best be described as idle and inconsequent. Or at least eccentric and a little mad.'

'I can't say I have quite got my bearings on all this.' As he spoke, Basil Snodgrass strolled forward into the corridor. He was a spare and loose-limbed man, who moved with an easy negligence which, even in the middle of this strange conversation, seemed wholly unaffected. 'There are a good many odd people around. A respectable female domestic, for instance, who seems to belong to Beddoes's stable, and who is said to have been rather roughly handled. Do you know whom I mean? She has some absurd name. Mrs Scrabblecoke, or something of that sort.'

'Mrs Gathercoal.'

'Ah, yes. And then there is the local doctor. It was natural to send for him. But there is the local parson as well. There can't have been much occasion for his offices – not with Adrian so absolutely and instantly killed.'

'The Professor had invited Dr Absolon to join him earlier. The idea was that he should be present to welcome your half-brother should he turn up.'

'Which he did – but to a welcome of a very different sort. And why ever *should* Adrian be expected – suddenly and in the middle of the night?'

'That might almost be called a long story.' There was a hint of impatience in Appleby's voice. 'Professor Snodgrass and Adrian Snodgrass had a kind of compact. May I say that there are one or two more important matters to get clear?'

'I'm very sure there are.'

'Then may I ask you one rather vital question?'

'Certainly you may.' For a moment Basil Snodgrass had looked startled. 'Fire ahead.'

'Good. Can you tell me, please, whether your half-brother was left-handed?'

A brief silence was produced by this totally unexpected question. It was as if Basil Snodgrass felt some obscure necessity to take its measure. But when he did reply it was emphatically enough.

'My dear sir, I haven't the slightest idea. Curious as it may seem, we scarcely knew each other.'

'But I can tell you!' David Anglebury, who had been silent again during these exchanges, broke in almost eagerly. 'You will think it strange that I can, since it's such a long time since I met my . . . since I met Mr Snodgrass. But I told you how nice he was. He played with me for a bit: cricket, and a few minutes' knock-up at tennis. I remember it all pretty vividly, as it happens.'

'That is most interesting.' Appleby gave the young man a quick smile. 'Well?'

'He was definitely left-handed. I am quite sure of it.'

'Oddly enough, I am quite sure of it too.'

Chapter Seventeen

There could be no doubt – Appleby was telling himself half an hour later – about the authenticity of Basil Snodgrass. He was even lurking among those minor Snodgrasses in *Who's Who*, over whose names Appleby could now see that he had let his eye too rapidly pass. Basil's, indeed, even more than Adrian's, might be called a fade-out career. At Oxford he had been President both of the Union and the OUDS, and shortly thereafter appeared to have been gaining some fame for himself as a racing motorist. But this versatility had clearly turned into a somewhat feckless trying out one thing after another, so that so far as public record went he had simply died away.

Appleby had returned to the library to conduct this small investigation, and it occurred to him to take another look at the handsome engraving over the fireplace of the Seat of Augustus Snodgrass Esquire. He could now see that it represented all four wings of the mansion as already in being, and that he could quite well trace out, if he wanted to, the course of his own nocturnal scamperings around the place. He was just reflecting that it made an admirable theatre for highly theatrical goings-on when the door opened and Dr Plumridge entered.

'I'm thinking of calling it a day,' Plumridge said, '– or rather a night. The police surgeon has arrived, and I propose leaving him to it. But I thought I'd seek you out and say good-bye.'

'That's very nice of you.' Appleby wondered whether Plumridge's civil impulse in fact meant that he had something to communicate. 'Would you say that the police surgeon has caught up with your own observations?'

'My own observations, Sir John?'

'You must forgive me. I just have a notion that you don't feel things to be precisely as they seem. The when and where of Adrian Snodgrass's killing, for example. And what he was doing when he was killed.'

'Ah.'

'I'd be grateful if you'd step over here' – Appleby had crossed the room – 'and look at this photograph. It is undoubtedly of Adrian as a small boy, and dressed up as a soldier. With some care and at some expense, you notice. He's rather like some little royal personage wearing the real thing.'

'Perfectly true.'

'I wonder whether it suggests or recalls to you a small physical fact about Adrian – something, as a matter of fact, that I've been seeking information on within the last hour.'

'The boy's right hand is resting on the hilt of his sword – which he has contrived to put on his right side. And that's irregular, without a doubt, from a military point of view. The child knows his left hand is, so to speak, his business hand. And he's a self-willed little devil, as one can see. So he has fixed things so that he can most effectively draw the sword, and wield it, left-handed. I don't positively recall Adrian as left-handed. But obviously he was so.'

'From which, Doctor, it follows . . .?'

'That somebody has been none too clever. A left-handed man, when surprised and alarmed, doesn't snatch up a poker in his right hand and go charging through the house with it. And, of course, there are one or two other things that make that macabre little tableau unconvincing.'

'Such as?'

'Rather too little blood *in situ*. Forensic medicine isn't quite a country G.P.'s province, and I don't propose to burden the professionals with flighty theories. But, since you ask me, Sir John, there it is. My bet would be that the initial haemorrhage took place elsewhere.'

'And earlier than the picture suggests?'

'Well, obviously – if a dead or dying man was dragged to where the body now lies. One can't determine a time of death all that accurately. But it clearly wasn't, say, early in the evening, or anything like it. Then there's the position of the body ...' Plumridge broke off. 'But you're drawing me into teaching you your own A.B.C.'

'Please go on.'

'If you came charging at me, and if I hit you very hard and square on the jaw, you would be much more likely to drop supine than prone. And a bullet, of course, is just such a blow – but packing a far greater impact still.'

'We ought to have found the body on its back?'

'It's no more than a probability, I'd say. The victim might turn or pivot as he fell, I suppose. Only in that case, and knowing the direction in which Adrian was running ...'

'Or has been represented as running.'

'Yes, of course. That's what we're talking about. If the thing were, so to speak, genuine, I'd have expected that the spin that brought the body down prone would have landed its heels in the drawing-room and its head in the hall.'

'I think you are right in that. So what does all this suggest?'

'Something that an amateur scarcely wants to be the first to go round airing.' Plumridge spoke soberly. 'The whole appearance of burglary, and so on, has been faked as a cloak for something quite different.'

'Well, yes.' Appleby looked speculatively at the doctor. 'I'm bound to say I almost convinced myself of that quite early on. But it won't do.' Appleby paused. 'You look relieved.'

'Do I? I suppose I am. One positively wants to feel that there have really been – well, professional criminals at work. Habitual criminals. You think there have been?'

'That, my dear Doctor, depends on how one defines one's terms.' Appleby was again silent for a moment. 'Can you spare a further minute or two? I have something to tell you, as a matter of fact.'

'But of course.' Plumridge sat down. 'Does it pick up, perhaps, from our last conversation? When we had a word or two, I mean, on the difficult problem of professional confidence.'

'Yes, indeed. But there was something that came before that. I was anxious to get hold of a very simple piece of information. Who was going to inherit Ledward now that Adrian was dead? It seemed scarcely plausible that the family doctor wouldn't know. But you struck me, if I may say so, as a little evasive. Indeed, you said something to the effect that you were not the family lawyer. Might I be right in thinking that what was operative was your sense that you knew who *ought* to inherit the place? Morally, I mean, as distinct from legally.'

'Um.'

'You can't be called exactly communicative, Doctor. So here is what I want to tell you. David Anglebury *has* been communicative. He has confided to me pretty well everything he appears to know about himself.'

'Then he is to be accounted a very sensible lad.'

'Thank you. He has mentioned that you were a great help to him at a time when he was trying to sort out his feelings about his father, and his father's conduct towards his mother. It isn't my impression, however, that you found it useful or possible at that time to give him any information which you may have possessed and he did not.'

'But what sort of information may I have possessed that would have been of any use to the boy?'

By this time, Doctor, it's rather a question of any information that may be of use to *me*. Here is young Anglebury – if we may call him that – faced with the very difficult situation created by his mother's wandering presence here at Ledward on this shocking night. He tells me that he is in fact the dead man's son, and that his mother has for a very long time cherished delusions – or what Anglebury judges to be delusions – about the circumstances attending the seduction which resulted in his birth. But he can hardly have any memories preserved from his earliest infancy, let alone any positively pre-natal ones. You, however, have explained to me that you have been in practice in this part of the country virtually throughout your working life, and you may very well have had the future Mrs Anglebury's misfortune more or less under your eye. You may even have delivered David into this world.'

'I did.'

'This is most encouraging. You are really becoming communicative.' Appleby glanced at Plumridge with a kind of whimsical irony. 'So what about the seduction? Did that happen under your eye as well?'

'My dear Sir John, I'm not, and never was, exactly a *voyeur*. But it's true I wasn't without information in the matter. Before she brought off – if that's not too gross a way of phrasing it – her rapid marriage to Charles Anglebury, the unfortunate woman had occasion to consult me.' Plumridge paused. 'Well, here *is* a professional confidence. She was pregnant, and she wanted to know whether there might not be something in the state of her health which would make the termination of the pregnancy desirable on medical grounds.'

'In other words, she was hoping you might get her out of her plight by arranging a quiet abortion?'

'Just that. Of course I explained the legal and ethical position to her as well and gently as I could.' Plumridge hesitated. 'She had a good deal more to say.'

'She told you this story of an outrageous piece of wickedness on Adrian Snodgrass's part? Of his having arranged, on some pretext, a secret marriage ceremony, which later turned out to be fraudulent and invalid?'

'Just that.'

'Do you agree with David that her persuasion can only have been a delusion, and that no educated woman could possibly be so deceived?'

'The answer to that must depend, you know, on the opinion one had formed of her pre-existing mental state. A woman who was simple-minded in the sense of being positively mentally subnormal ...'

138

'But there was no question of that?'

'Definitely not. On the other hand, I think it would be fair enough to say that she was already a little off her head. But you see how that may bear upon the matter in quite contradictory ways.'

'I'm not sure that I understand you.'

'She would be the more ready simply to *imagine* things; say to bring into being, and genuinely believe in, the melodramatic fantasy of a mock-marriage by way of providing an excuse for what she was certainly conventional enough to think of as her fall.'

'The authentic Victorian vision.'

'Yes. And I must point out, Sir John, that, unlike you, I am literally a Victorian myself. So I'm not sure there isn't something to be said for that very simple point of view. However, I come to the other way of regarding the problem. If she was already a little mad – as I believe she was – it *might* be the easier actually to put her under a false persuasion. An educated woman in a normal state of mind, that is to say, would be likely to penetrate such a deception, however cleverly arranged. But think of her as disturbed, or as on the verge of requiring custodial care, and the particular piece of wickedness we are wondering about does become feasible.'

'Are you then telling me, Doctor, that one guess is as good as another? Short of successful investigation of actual events which occurred a full generation ago, we can never know whether Adrian Snodgrass's possessing himself of this unhappy woman was accomplished by means of a criminal deception or not?'

'I'm not saying that at all.' Dr Plumridge had risen a little stiffly from his chair. He was an old man, and had been through a long night. 'Why not ask the lady for a little more information?'

'Ask the lady!' For a moment Appleby was simply astonished.

'Certainly. Now.'

'But isn't she asleep?'

'She has been. But I don't believe in narcosis in a big way. Mrs Anglebury is in a room upstairs, very tolerably awake, and no doubt thinking up the extraordinary things she's going to tell the police. I'd get in first, if I were you.'

'My dear sir, is there any point in its being *me* who has the extraordinary things fired at him?'

'Reason in madness, Sir John. Every psychiatrist – every mad-doctor, as my generation says – is looking for just that. And you can't have spent your professional life at grips with the criminal mind without having become a bit of a mad-doctor yourself.'

'Very well,' Appleby said. 'And I'm obliged to you.'

Chapter Eighteen

When Appleby made his way upstairs to seek out the unfortunate Mrs Anglebury – whom he hoped to find refreshed and even composed – it was with a sense of leisure and security, neither of which feelings he was to look back upon as well founded.

He had, indeed, substantial reasons for confidence. His watch told him it was half-past five. This meant that, if he were to emerge from Ledward (still so extensively and expensively illuminated) and penetrate some way into the darkness of the park, it would almost certainly be possible to distinguish a first faint intimation of light in the eastern sky. But it was still a long time till breakfast. He had made, moreover, in his inner mind, very reasonable speed in elucidating the mysterious affair he had so casually intruded upon. To the very core of it, it might be said, he had penetrated within something like two seconds of its having become possible to do so. There had been nothing miraculous about this. He had been on plenty of such trails before, and must be accounted an old hound and a sagacious one, with a developed sense of smell. That, and a capacity for listening, had constituted the only witchcraft he had used. And it didn't seem to him that, essentially, there was much more he needed to know. It was true that he had discerned one odd possibility the confirmation of which might radically alter the final issue of the whole deplorable business. But there was no sign of its being a possibility which had entered any other living head, and he would assuredly – so to speak – keep it firmly under his own hat until he had found means to determine on it one way or another.

Certainly neither life nor property appeared any longer at risk at Ledward. Unless, of course, his own life. He alone, it might be, was in a position to identify the sinister foreigner with the drooping moustache – a gentleman who, whatever his own unlawful concerns at Ledward may have been, was probably aware that he had been uncomfortably in the vicinity of homicide. He alone (with all respect to Inspector Stride) might be conceived by one interested party or another as the man who knew too much. And he didn't feel entitled wholly to neglect action appropriate to this situation. But the main point was that the riddle of Adrian Snodgrass's death was now getting itself answered with reasonable speed.

This was why, on his way upstairs (and not perhaps without a touch of that hazardous attitude known to students of Greek drama as *hubris*), he paused to confirm himself in the view that the flowing curves around him could represent the conception only of Robert Adam himself. The constable who had been detailed to guide him to Mrs Anglebury watched this gesture of connoisseurship with respect. He was no doubt under the impression that the great man was looking for fingerprints or blood-stains in unexpected places.

Professor Beddoes Snodgrass's devoted care of Ledward Park, and his anxiety that it should present itself as a going concern to his nephew Adrian upon whatever birthday anniversary he should choose to turn up, had not extended to giving an appearance of present occupation to the secondary bedrooms of the house. In the chamber in which Mrs Anglebury was resting everything rollable had been rolled up, everything swathable swathed, and everything baggable tied firmly into bags. Cats in bags, Appleby thought as he glanced around. Enormous cats in enormous bags, waiting to be let out. And he wondered whether the lady had, as it were, a further cat in a bag tucked up her sleeve.

She was reclining on a bare mattress, but had been provided with an eiderdown quilt, plenty of pillows, and a cheerful-looking electric fire. And if she didn't herself look cheerful, at least she looked calm. She might also have been described as remaining more handsome than ravaged. Adrian Snodgrass's way with women had doubtless been reprehensible. But his taste had been good.

'Good morning,' Appleby said. 'My name is Appleby. You may recall that we met last night.'

'Yes, of course.' Appleby's words, which had struck him as absurd even as he uttered them, didn't seem to discompose Mrs Anglebury in the least. 'Not when I was on top of a bed, as I am now, but when I was under one. Did I tell you I had killed Adrian?'

'Yes, Mrs Anglebury, you did.'

'I get things wrong sometimes. I rather think I got that wrong.'

'You will find others who agree with you in that.'

'Because, you know, *why* was I under the bed? I must have been hiding from Adrian. In other words, it was Adrian who was trying to kill me. Which clears the matter up.'

'As a matter of fact, you said at the time that you were hiding from some men. Not from Adrian, Mrs Anglebury. From some men you didn't like the look of. And you weren't imagining them. You really did see them. I myself saw them too.' Although thus expressing things as simply as he could, Appleby found himself without much hope of making any progress with David Anglebury's mother. For here in front of him was something not in the least like the wayward battiness and obscure wilfulness or disingenuousness of the aged Professor Snodgrass. Mrs Anglebury was insane. It had been absurd of Dr Plumridge to suggest that a layman, whatever degree of mental eccentricity his career had brought him in contact with, could get anything useful out of her.

'For a long time,' Mrs Anglebury continued, 'Adrian was simply trying to have me put away. He had enlisted powerful support. The Prime Minister was in the plot. And of course – and as you might guess – the Archbishop of Canterbury. But Monsieur Picasso stood out. It was very much to his credit. They wanted him to paint me so that I should look mad, and then they were going to show the painting to the Queen. I was to have two eyes in the middle of my left cheek. This would have the effect of making me look strange. But I foiled all their attempts. That is why Adrian started trying to kill me.' She paused, and smoothed the eiderdown over her knees. 'Do I make myself clear?'

'I think it may be said that you do.' Appleby was by now simply wondering how he could retrieve this painful false step and get away. For here was a degree of helpless alienation which it was merely indecent to intrude upon.

'Adrian and I were married,' Mrs Anglebury said, 'on the 21st of January 1953, in the parish church of St Botolph's, Oxford.'

'I beg your pardon?' Appleby, who had seated himself at a cautious remove from the demented lady, sat up with a jerk. 'Do I understand . . .'

'It was because of its being a runaway match.' Mrs Anglebury had been heedless of interruption. 'And Adrian, you see, was very fond of Oxford – although his career there had not been so successful as that of his half-brother Basil, whom I have no doubt that you know. And of course the Vicar of St Botolph's, who performed the ceremony, was an old friend of Adrian's. In fact, he had been the chaplain of his college. The Reverend Frederick Templeman, M.A.'

'I see. Do you recall whether the banns were called in a regular way, or whether the marriage was by special . . .'

'Yes, by special licence. It was from the Archbishop of Canterbury.'

'Never mind about the Archbishop,' Appleby said hastily. 'And what happened then?'

'Then? We set out on a short wedding-journey on the continent. But, no – that is not quite correct. We were *about* to set out on such a journey. To Venice. We had neither of us ever been to Venice.'

'And then something disconcerting happened?'

'Disconcerting? I don't think so.' Mrs Anglebury shook her head vaguely. It was as if she were losing interest in the discussion. 'I wonder whether it is possible to ring for early morning tea in this hotel?'

'Well, there is a respectable person – a Mrs Gathercoal – who I hope may be induced to bring you some. But you were telling me about your marriage.'

'Was I? Charles and I were married – if my memory is correct – in the spring of 1953.'

'Your memory is certainly correct. But we were speaking of your marriage not to Charles Anglebury, but to Adrian Snodgrass.'

'That wasn't a marriage at all.' Mrs Anglebury's voice had changed suddenly; it was as if she was back in the region she had been inhabiting when this strange conversation opened. 'Not a marriage at all,' she repeated. 'Mr Templeman, you see, hadn't been Mr Templeman – only some wicked friend of Adrian's. It had all been contrived so that I might be undone.' Mrs Anglebury paused on this archaic word, and appeared to take satisfaction in it. 'Undone,' she repeated.

'This is something you remember discovering shortly after what you thought had been a true wedding ceremony?'

'I didn't discover it. Adrian told me.'

'After you had been living together for a little time? After a quarrel, perhaps?'

'Perhaps after a quarrel. But I think perhaps it was after I had been having some of my funny turns. He didn't like them.'

'Mrs Anglebury, I wonder whether I have got this right? Adrian simply told you that you were not legally his wife, that he had no intention of making you so, and that you had better clear out, keep quiet, and manage as best you could?'

'Yes. Of course, it was all long before he started wanting to kill me. Or was it that I started wanting to kill him? I think you and I were talking about that. But I forget.'

'Never mind that for a moment. There is something I want to know.' Appleby had stood up, and was now standing over Mrs Anglebury as if a further brief sanity could be compelled upon her by sheer effort of will. 'After your ... your relationship with Adrian Snodgrass – with David's father – broke up, did you ever see Adrian again?'

'Oh, yes. But only once. It was when David was a small boy. Adrian must have been staying at Ledward. That's the

Snodgrasses' family place, and I don't think it can be far from this hotel . . . I wonder if you would be so kind as to ring for that tea?'

'It will be coming very soon. You say you encountered Adrian?'

'Yes. I was walking in the park at Ledward. It is something I sometimes do. And somebody was shooting rabbits, or perhaps it was pigeons. It turned out to be Adrian.' Mrs Anglebury's limbs were now moving restlessly, spasmodically beneath the eiderdown. 'We talked.'

'Was David mentioned?'

'Yes – because, you see, somehow or other Adrian had met him. I think he had liked him very much.'

'Yes?'

'But not me. I could feel that I horrified him. I can't think why. But it was almost as if it was the way I talked.'

There was a silence. It represented Appleby seeking cautiously for words. He was on the verge – but only on the verge – of confirming his own strangest notion of the Ledward affair.

'Mrs Anglebury – how did the conversation end?'

'It was about something being mended.' Mrs Anglebury's head moved strangely. She might have been trying to see round the corner of a veil, a darkness, a mist. 'No. It was about something that couldn't be mended.'

'Never?'

'Not in Adrian's lifetime – or at least not for years ahead. He said that one day he might become a stronger man than he was then. But of course he *was* strong. He liked to show it sometimes with the men – tossing sheaves or hauling at a rope. So it must have been something *really* difficult to mend. Do you think it might have had to do with a tractor, or with one of the bridges over the River Ledward where it runs through the park?'

'These are obviously possibilities. But did Adrian say anything more about it?'

'He said something about papers. That there were papers securely tucked away at Ledward which would put things straight one day.'

'I see.' Appleby stood up as he uttered these far from idle

145

words. 'I'm bound to say that Adrian Snodgrass strikes me as a penitent of a distinctly procrastinating sort.'

'I wonder whether David has caught the burglars.'

'What's that?' It had been for his own satisfaction that Appleby had uttered his last grim reflection, and he had been obliged to recall himself to Mrs Anglebury with a jerk. 'What was that you said?'

'David was with me here until a few minutes before you arrived. But then this man came in and whispered to him. I think I wasn't supposed to hear. But I did.'

'What man was this, Mrs Anglebury? Try to tell me.'

'I don't know. But he said he knew who the burglars were, and he and David could corner them on their own if they were quick. So he took David away.'

'You are sure this whispering man was a stranger to you?'

'Well, not quite. I mean he did seem vaguely familiar.'

'It wasn't Professor Snodgrass?'

'Oh, no. I should know Professor Snodgrass at once. Even if he suddenly turned up in this hotel.'

'A man stinking of soap and heaven knows what?'

'I shouldn't notice. I smoke too much. Have you any cigarettes?'

'No, I have not. Try to remember anything more.'

'There wasn't anything more – except that the man took David into a corner of the room where I couldn't hear what he said. Or only the bit about the park.'

'And what was that?'

'That he knew the crooks had a hide-out there, and would be lying low until they could get away. And David nodded, and they both ran out of the room.'

'Damnation!' Uttering this surprising expletive, Appleby strode first to the bedroom door, where he flicked off the lights, and then swiftly to the window. Heavy curtains had been drawn across it, and he flung these back and gazed out.

A thin grey light of dawn hovered in the park – a light still so faint that it might have been no more than a slow evaporation from the grey moisture of the grass. It would almost have been possible to interpret these scant visual evidences as a seascape in which a single dark tree showed like a becalmed galleon with inken sails presaging doom. But the sea was parting even as Appleby looked; it was rolling itself up into shapeless bundles as if in imitation of the swathed and shrouded objects inside this room; in places these little bundles were beginning to move with the slow deliberation of grazing sheep, or to disintegrate and fade like small clouds unable to withstand the sun. But there was as yet no sun here. For as much as another half-hour, perhaps, the park at Ledward would be a theatre of opening and closing vistas, drifting vapours, obstinately lingering shades.

Appleby threw open the window, and for a moment stood listening. Seemingly far away – although it might not be far away at all – he thought he heard voices calling: the voices, perhaps, of two men who had lost contact with each other and were seeking to regain it.

Without so much as pausing to shut the window again, Appleby turned and ran from the room.

Chapter Nineteen

There were no thoughts of Robert Adam in Appleby's head this time as he tumbled himself dangerously down the elegant main staircase of Ledward Park. In the hall he scribbled a note and then shouted directions to a policeman, but didn't pause to see with what speed this mustered support behind him. He had no doubt whatever of the particular dire hazard which had suddenly presented itself, and no disposition to deny that in his assessment of the situation he had failed to take account of the one bizarre possibility that might lead to it. So it was very much up to him to move quickly now.

When he emerged from the house it was momentarily into an effect of darkness, but this was only because he had been passing once more through that oppressively over-illuminated interior. As his vision accommodated itself he saw that the columns of the great portico outside the front door stood dark against a sky faintly flushed with rose, and as he dropped down the elaborately balustraded stone steps to the level of the gardens and the drive he received an impression that daylight was farther advanced than he had supposed.

But there was another factor at work, and of this he became aware as soon as he had negotiated a ha-ha and entered the park itself. The morning mist which from the height of Mrs Anglebury's window had suggested no more than the thickness of a blanket on the ground was in fact a shifting and opaque integument in places more than head-high. And the little fleecy sheep which had appeared to move grazing over the surface of this chilly pasture were tall enough to envelop whole trees for a time in a magic cloak of invisibility.

Appleby paused to listen. In these conditions – familiar only to those who go abroad at dawn – sound might be muted too, and any quarter from which it did come not easy to be certain of. But at least he did again hear voices, although they sounded far away. So he set off again at a run. There was now a broad stream on his left hand. Presumably it was the River Ledward to which Mrs Anglebury had referred in one of her more rambling moments. A couple of herons were standing in the water; their heads rotated with the suggestion of some malign scanning mechanism as they watched Appleby go by. He turned his own head and glanced behind him. There was no sign of any of Stride's men.

And there was no sign of Ledward either. As if it really were the monstrous scurrying crustacean of Appleby's earlier fantasy, it had picked itself up and vanished. But what had really happened, of course, was that mist and indeed fog, far from progressively dispersing before the cheerful sun as had at first appeared, were now in fact billowing into the park with the sudden exuberance of foam from a fire-extinguisher. Appleby hadn't a sufficient sense of the emergency confronting him – or not, at least, in its likely detail – to be confident whether there was advantage or disadvantage in this change. At least he himself was now depending wholly on sound for the opportunity to be of any effectiveness at all. But then the same circumstance could equally impair the operations of others as well. And probably this sudden effect of what astronauts call visibility degradation would last no more than a few minutes.

There was now only one voice calling, and it still seemed to come from straight ahead of him. It was David Anglebury's voice, and it was repeatedly calling out a name – the name of Snodgrass. Was it Basil, or was it the Professor who was thus being conjured to reveal himself?

Appleby didn't think it made much difference.

And then – hard upon this thought – came the crisis. David's voice was still to be heard, but had grown fainter. It was much as if he had taken a wrong cast in the childrens' game known as 'Hot and Cold'. Appleby had briefly to debate whether to give the young man a shout himself – since to call him to heel, so to speak, would be a desirable measure in face of what was afoot. On the other hand, to give such a shout was to announce himself as an intrusive presence upon whatever was going forward. So Appleby decided to accept a further measure of risk, and thus maintain himself as an unknown factor in the proceedings.

He came abruptly to a halt, and in another instant was prone in wet chill grass. The vapour had parted in front of him, to reveal a low stone wall (no more, indeed, than the vestige of a wall, now no longer with any function) which ran down a gentle slope towards the stream. It was behind the shelter of this that he was flat on his tummy now. Beyond it, he had glimpsed a dim light – whether of torch or lantern – which mysteriously suggested itself as in some way buried in the earth. And, from the same enigmatical quarter, there came a murmur of voices. They were voices speaking in a foreign tongue.

This last was a circumstance by which Appleby might be said to have been favourably impressed.

The place was an ice-house. It was this not in the loose modern sense of an environment very much colder than is comfortable, but literally and technically. Here, in fact, was one of those caverns, dug into conveniently rising ground and provided with such insulating walls as our rude forefathers could devise, in which, for the use of great houses like Ledward, ice was formerly stored throughout the year. A century might

have passed since this particular ice-house had been function-
ing; gardeners or a gamekeeper might have used it since; its
entrance was now so overgrown as to suggest a long period
of absolute desuetude. It was a good hide-out. It would be a
handy place in which to tuck away objects which there might
be awkwardness in being found in possession of.

'Snodgrass?'

Appleby glanced up, to find David Anglebury standing beside him in the mist. He could see that the young man was in
a state of high excitement.

'Oh – I thought you were Basil Snodgrass. I got separated
from him. He and I have been . . .' David broke off. 'Listen!'

'*David, get down!*'

'Spanish . . . it's them!' David had sprung forward, thereby
unconsciously eluding a ruthless sweep which Appleby had
aimed at his legs. 'We've got them . . . come on!'

The young man was over the wall – he had taken it like a
hurdle almost from a standing start – and was charging the
ice-house much as if it represented a pair of goal-posts and he
had a rugger-ball under his arm. Appleby, fortunately already
on his feet, managed a fairly rapid vault. He gave another warning shout, but it was of no avail. Perhaps the young idiot
took it for encouragement – as a kind of hunting cry. There
was nothing for it but for Appleby to get up a quite improbable speed. And this – it was for no more than a few yards,
all told – he did in some miraculous manner achieve. The young
man with an imaginary rugger-ball was brought abruptly to
earth by a far from imaginary tackle. In the same instant there
was the crack of a pistol from dead ahead. Appleby was aware
of it as a good shot. The bullet had passed through empty air
which, a split second before, was being displaced by David's
flying body.

As it happened, the grass was long, and the ground broken,
so that some sort of minimal cover was not hard to find. There
was still a light – it might have been designed as a little bea-
con – in the ice-house; and it was to this that Appleby might
now have been conceived as addressing himself in unemotional tones.

'That was it,' Appleby said. 'The last boss-shot in a

pathetically incompetent affair. Ingenious in places, yes. But well-conceived, no. And it won't be any good now having a go at hunting us down. The police will be trotting up at any minute. and we could dodge you, off our own bats, for an hour. Nor am I the only man who now knows the facts of the case. I took the precaution of making a progress report to somebody – I won't name him – from which the whole set-up can certainly be worked out. So – as I said – that was it. Finish.'

Silence greeted this speech. The only sound was a faint rustle in the grass, and in trees which seconds ago had been invisible, but which now showed as dark, crag-like islands from which a milky sea-spray was falling away. The vapours were departing. The entrance to the ice-house revealed itself as a mouldering wooden door on broken hinges. It was rather a pitiful refuge.

Suddenly there was a second shot – so that Appleby threw an arm round David's shoulders and forced him farther to the ground. Then, almost immediately, there was a third. Immediately, and from somewhere still in mist on the right, a small hubbub arose. It might have been the police, emerging, in a belated but spectacular fashion, and with much banging of doors and stamping of feet, from some unsuspected hiding-place near by. Appleby didn't turn his head. Herons behave like that when getting under way. Here were simply two or three more, justly alarmed, hastily quitting some invisible plantation and proposing to join their fellows in the water.

It was for something else that Appleby was listening: for so much as a single cry or moan from the direction of the ice-house. Nothing. Nothing came from the place except a small drift of vapour darker than the pearl-grey mist now everywhere in retreat from the park; except this, and a faint acrid smell.

Appleby stood up.

'A very old-fashioned weapon,' he said. 'Could it even be a double-action Colt?' He paused, and looked appraisingly at the boy now scrambling to his feet beside him. 'I'm afraid it might be a good idea if we went in there together. The spectacle mayn't be very agreeable, but that would be the best course from the point of view of giving evidence later on. Do you mind, Snodgrass?'

'No – although I think I know what we're going to find.' Although very pale, the young man took a brisk pace forward. Then he paused. '*Snodgrass?*' he repeated.

'The truth is as you can't but have imagined it at times. Snodgrass has never been other than your true name. And – since very early this morning – Ledward has belonged to you.'

Chapter Twenty: *Epilogue*

'An excellent woman, Mrs Gathercoal,' Dr Absolon said, a few hours later. He was walking with Appleby across the park, preparatory to offering him the hospitality of Ledward Vicarage. It was from this undisturbed abode, it had been agreed, that the rescue of Appleby's car might be effected with a minimum of publicity. 'To organize coffee and bacon-and-eggs after a night like that was a considerable feat. Not to speak of the capital potted char. A most interesting old-world dish.' Absolon paused. 'But it is hardly surprising that young David had little appetite. It must all be a terrific shock to him. Particularly as it culminated in finding the bodies of poor Beddoes and the scoundrel Basil.'

'Each was as great a scoundrel as the other, Vicar.'

'But surely Beddoes was a mere accomplice, and more than a little mad?'

'To my mind, nothing of the kind. When I tumbled in on the middle of their plot last night, the Professor may be said to have put on a very distinguished turn indeed. He was as good an actor, in a way, as the fellow one is inclined to call Basil-Leonidas. And Basil had, at least as a young man, actual experience as an actor.'

'Indeed?'

'Well, as an amateur and when at Oxford. See *Who's Who*. But when he returned to the scene of action so hard upon removing Leonidas's beard, it ought to have occurred to him not to stink of soap and what they call after-shave lotion.'

'It was really so odd a circumstance that alerted you?'

'Well, say that I was at once aware of it – having a good sense of smell.' Appleby smiled. 'But really, the instant he entered the corridor, I remember simply staring in astonishment at the effrontery of the proposed deception. They were very rash, to put it mildly, to go ahead with their plan once they knew the identity of the stranger out of the night.'

'Yourself, you mean?'

'Precisely. My wits may be growing dim, but I'm a professional, after all. You see, as the thing was plotted, it would be only yourself – called in to substantiate the story of lurking and implausibly chattering thieves – who would be likely to see the briskly materializing Basil hard upon the departure of the offended Leonidas. It was all entirely foolish, nevertheless. Particularly as almost the same complicated preparations must have been made last year – and would have been next year, one has to suppose, if Adrian hadn't turned up last night.'

'Yet, basically, their plan was fairly simple.'

'Perfectly true. In the interest of Basil, who would succeed to the property and then do a quiet share-out with Beddoes, Adrian was to be killed as soon as he turned up, and the blame laid on non-existent burglars. But they elaborated far too much – simply, I suppose, in a spirit of malign and rejoicing ingenuity. The interrupted supper and the clutched poker. All those sound effects – a little lacking, incidentally, in lucid sequence – which were a mere matter of time-clocks and magnetic tape.

'Not that it wasn't all marvellously dextrous. Basil must have done an uncommon amount of brisk skipping around before he presented himself to Beddoes and myself. "Mr Snodgrass is in residence", forsooth! His manoeuvres had included, remember, the actual intercepting and shooting of Adrian when still out of earshot. What Beddoes would call terrain and tactics, no doubt.'

'Ah, that admirable book.'

'But there was one staring indication of the bogus character of the off-stage noises. Out on the terrace, Basil tried out one sequence – simply to test it, I imagine – in what happened to be my hearing during my first unsuspected presence in the library. It was the one of the thieves chattering or whispering, dropping something metallic, and then making off at the double. You got the benefit of it as you came through the park. But I'd heard the rehearsal. The identical sequence twice over! There could be only one explanation of that.'

'God bless my soul!'

'But they were both capable of quick thinking. When they got at the truth about David . . .'

'I don't understand that at all.'

'I'll explain in a moment. But, when they did, and saw that *he* must appear to be killed by intruders as well, they did a really brilliant improvisation. Voices again – but real voices this time. In fact their own voices, talking Spanish. They had to reckon, having set their trap, that they might fail to kill the boy, or somehow be surprised, and have to bolt. There would then have been David's own testimony that it had been our Latin-American friends who had been for some mysterious reason gunning for him.'

'But there really *have* been . . .'

'Oh, indeed yes. And the reason I wasn't very briskly backed up by the police in the crisis was that they had got word of them and were after them. Our friends from Azuera had crashed the car they were escaping in, and had scattered. So it required quite a force to bring them in. It was effected pretty quickly, all the same. And it is pretty quickly, too, that these South American gentry have tumbled out their story. It has been the wisest thing they could do.' Appleby halted for a moment. The herons were still in the water, and their heads were still behaving like automata. 'They *had* arrived to do a little buglary . . .'

'Which was a most absurd coincidence.'

'Not really. They had to beat Adrian to it, so to speak, and they just brought it off. Of course they proved to have been under a comical misconception, so that in the end they simply dropped everything, and ran. *Literally* dropped everything. And that, I have to confess, was something I didn't reckon on. And my stupidity nearly cost young David his life.'

'My dear Appleby, I am quite bewildered. You speak in riddles.'

'Nothing of the kind, Vicar. I am explaining this rather odd affair to you at breakneck speed, and with a lucidity born of years of practice.' Appleby looked half-seriously at Dr Absolon. 'Ask me any question whatever, and I'll carry on logically from that point.'

It was some moments before Dr Absolon availed himself of this invitation. He too had halted, and was studying the creatures hunched in the shallows of the Ledward.

'God has not died for the white heron,' he said. 'God has not appeared to the birds.'

'I beg your pardon?'

'I'm sorry. Only a modern poet's way of raising an interesting theological point. But here's your question. What did those foreigners want from a safe, and how did they know it was there?'

'Two questions, Vicar, but both quite simple ones. Long ago, Adrian Snodgrass let it be known that he had somewhere tucked away documents the production of which would at any time be fatal to some political group or other in Azuera. And at this point we have to rely a little upon what those people's emissaries (as I suppose they should be called) told Stride after he'd hauled them in this morning. It seems that Adrian, quite recently and just before setting out for England, hit the bottle in what proved to be politically unreliable company. He was coming back to Ledward, he announced in his cups, to get some papers out of a safe hidden behind the portrait of a lady in his bedroom – and the consequences were to be of a highly dramatic order. That's why, as I said a couple of minutes ago, our recent visitors had to beat Adrian to it. It was their job to find the safe, blow it, check the documents, and then either carry them off or destroy them.'

'And they succeeded?'

'They did, up to a point – and, although their investigation proved a fiasco, they might have got clean away had they not been a bit shaken and run into a tree.'

'A fiasco? The incriminating documents weren't there?'

'They weren't there. Probably they had never been there.

Possibly Adrian had dropped the notion of political revenge, and destroyed them long ago. What was there was a certificate of marriage. I've never seen it, and I suppose that now I never shall. But I can give you the names, the date, and the church. The officiating clergyman was a Mr Templeman. You see, Mrs Anglebury – not that she has any title to be called that – can be much more precisely communicative at moments than her unfortunate condition of mind would suggest.'

'In fact the lad we call David Anglebury is the legitimate son . . .?'

'Precisely. It was an obscure possibility to be reckoned with from early on. Indeed, you may recall my putting it to you. The marriage between his mother and Adrian Snodgrass was perfectly valid. But the lady quickly proved so dotty that Adrian lost his nerve, and got clear of her by telling her a perfectly ghastly lie. It seems incredible that he got away with it. But the whole thing had been a secret and runaway affair, which presumably made the deception feasible. *She* believed *him*. Then, later, nobody much bothered to believe *her*. Much later still, Adrian met his son, and liked him. His conscience got to work – only it wasn't a conscience of a particularly expeditious order.'

'It would by no means have been necessary that he should produce that scrap of paper from the safe in order to prove the validity of the marriage and to effect the legitimation of his son.'

'Perfectly true. But he wanted to do the thing in style. Or even, you might say, with a touch of theatre. The Snodgrasses (as Basil-Leonidas had the effrontery to tell me about himself) have a theatrical streak to them. But now I come, Vicar, to a fantastic turn in the affair. Adrian is dead: successfully killed by the bogus butler, and his body disposed according to plan. But our South American friends are still hanging on grimly – and Beddoes Snodgrass actually encounters or glimpses them. Coming after the jar of *my* appearance, it was almost too much for the old rascal. He could only call weakly for Leonidas – in other words for Basil, who was undoubtedly the initiating and controlling intelligence all through. The South Americans, I say, hang on grimly, and blow the safe. They see at once that the only document it contains is totally without significance for them. So they simply chuck it away, and bolt.'

'*Chuck it away*?'

'Yes. And one of our two native worthies – Beddoes or Basil – finds it. That was the bizarre circumstance that beat me. They realized that, if their whole elaborate course of criminality was not to be in vain, David Snodgrass must follow his father Adrian Snodgrass rapidly into the grave.'

'But if they had simply destroyed the marriage certificate . . .'

'No good at all. The discovery that David was legitimate, and heir to the estate, was a thoroughly shattering one. They knew, after all, that their evil star had brought me to Ledward. They knew I would heard about Mrs Anglebury's supposed delusions regarding a false marriage. And they knew that, having stumbled upon a mysterious crime, I wouldn't let so dubious a piece of past history go uninvestigated. Even if the poor woman hadn't come out with date and place as she did, a little organized police investigation would have got at the records. Ledward was as good as David's – unless David went.'

'They might have been disposed to feel that you ought to go too.'

'That's true. But before going off on that final chase I scribbled three words – just three – for the excellent inspector Stride. They might have puzzled him for a minute or two. But finally they'd have taken him right to the end of the road.'

'*Three* words?'

'*Basil was Leonidas.*'

'A succinct communication, indeed. But about a most complicated affair! From what would you be inclined to say that it all *began*?'

'From the open house – the rather fantastic birthday compact which must once have been simply a light-hearted affair between Adrian Snodgrass and an uncle who didn't like him nearly so much as he imagined. It was the legendary tryst that brought David's mother here – and the lad himself after her. It was the same legendary tryst that must have set Basil's mind working. He would see that any reasonable police force would positively expect burglary, missing Claudes and so on under such conditions – and would take an enraged house-holder shot by panic-stricken crooks as something entirely in order. He worked from that.'

'He was, in fact, a brilliant crook himself.'

'Oh, dear me – no!' The tone in which Appleby said this was almost shocked. 'The idea of a butler who couldn't be caught for the very good reason that he didn't exist, and who moreover had an unbreakable alibi because he was in the presence of witnesses when what would be taken to have been the fatal shot was heard: all that was ingenious enough, I agree. But Coxing and Boxing between two identities – at least intermittently – over a substantial period of time had nothing to commend it except the degree of virtuosity required. And his noises off – all that fun with tape-recorders and time-switches – was just a shade at random, as I've said. The woman's scream puzzled me, by the way. Why should he feed in that? But of course that was *real*: a *vica-voce* interpolation, so to speak, by our crazy lady.'

'You mentioned the Claude. Do you think it will have come to harm?'

'Almost certainly not. I have no doubt that Basil-Leonidas simply made off with it, and the rest of the supposed spoils, when I so trustingly instructed him to drive away and find a doctor. My guess is that the Campagna with Banditti will be safely in Stride's keeping by sundown.'

'We cross this foot-bridge,' Dr Absolon said presently, 'and it is the gate of my back-garden that is in front of us. You must excuse the state of the lawns. The leaves have begun to fall rather fast, you know, and I have been tardy in sweeping them up. Naturally I don't keep a gardener. But one or two of the pensioners among my parishioners are very good. They give me a hand from time to time, and with no thought of pay.'

'You must let me do the same, while waiting to hear about my confounded car.' Appleby paused, as his companion had done, to view the vicarage now before them. It was a house of very modest dimensions.

'I am extremely fortunate in my quarters,' Absolon said.

'Thatch is always picturesque. But it is also an admirable insulating agent. And that saves fuel.' He was silent, and then glanced at Appleby as if a fresh thought had struck him. 'I hope that Ledward, and the substantial wealth behind it, will not be too much for our young man. It need not necessarily be a blessing, I fear. And it is not as if he had been brought up to expectations of anything of the kind.'

'David Snodgrass will keep his head, I'd say. Or at least recover it quickly, even if it goes a little astray for a time.'

'He could, of course, do much good in the parish.' The vicar had moved forward again. Perhaps it was being on his own ground, Appleby thought, that was prompting him to these very proper professional reflections. 'It would be pleasant to feel that blessing might eventually come from these sad, and largely evil, events. But have you considered, my dear Sir John, their sober irony? It was a very wicked deed on Adrian Snodgrass's part that set all this in train years ago. But it was an eventual good impulse, an impulse to repent and make amends, that directly brought about his death.'

'Very true. But we must not be too hard even on his original course of conduct. The act of perfidy towards the distraught woman he had rashly run away with and married was of course abominable. But he must quite quickly have come to judge it too late for repentance. For Charles Anglebury appeared, a respectable seeming-marriage took place, and Adrian's child had a father. Within a few months of his sin – for it was a sin – he may have felt that telling the truth could produce only misery and scandal. I have some some sympathy with Adrian. But Beddoes and Basil are another matter.'

'Not wholly another matter. They must come together in our prayers. May God have mercy on their souls, all three.' Dr Absolon had opened a door, and now stood aside for Appleby to pass. 'I wonder,' he said, 'whether Mrs Gathercoal might be persuaded to give my housekeeper the receipt for that potted char?'

Michael Innes

'Mr Innes can write any other detective novelist out of sight. His books will stand reading again and again' – *Time and Tide*

'The most able writer of grotesque fantasy in crime fiction' – *Birmingham Post*

'Mr Innes engages the fourteen-year-old in high-brows' – T. C. Worsley on the B.B.C.

'A master – he constructs a plot that twists and turns like an electric eel: it gives you shock upon shock and you cannot let go' – *The Times Literary Supplement*

'The intellectual, the phantasmagoric, the exhilarating Mr Innes' – *Church Times*

The following Penguins by Michael Innes are available

Appleby at Allington

Appleby on Ararat

Appleby's End

A Connoisseur's Case

The Daffodil Affair

Death At The Chase

Family Affair

The Long Farewell

Money From Holme

The New Sonia Wayward

The Secret Vanguard